WOODS, Sara, pseud.

Tarry and be hanged. N.Y., Holt [1971, c1969]
184p. (A Rinehart suspense novel)

I. tc.

Tarry and Be Hanged

A RINEHART SUSPENSE NOVEL

A RINEHART SUSPENSE NOVEL

Tarry and Be Hanged

SARA WOODS

HOLT, RINEHART AND WINSTON
New York Chicago San Francisco

Fiction

Any work of fiction whose characters were of uniform excellence would rightly be condemned—by that fact if by no other—as being incredibly dull. Therefore no excuse can be considered necessary for the villainy or folly of the people appearing in this book. It seems extremely unlikely that any one of them should resemble a real person, alive or dead. Any such resemblance is completely unintentional and without malice.

First printed in the United States in 1971

Library of Congress Catalog Card Number: 77-150970

First Edition

SBN: 03-086022-9

Designer: Nancy Tausek
Printed in the United States of America

KING EDWARD:

Huntsman, what sayst thou? wilt thou go along?

HUNTSMAN:

Better do so than tarry and be hanged.

King Henry VI, Part 3, Act IV, Sc. 5

Tarry
and Be
Hanged

A RINEHART SUSPENSE NOVEL 

Part One

Easter Term,
1965

Wednesday, 19th May

The papers came into chambers in the ordinary way, and old Mr. Mallory (who had already heard from the managing clerk to the firm of solicitors concerned that the question of fees was not likely to cause any difficulty) made no more than a routine show of reluctance before he admitted cautiously that Mr. Maitland might be able to take the brief. But even Mr. Mallory, a stickler for the Way Things Are Done, would have shown no surprise to learn that Geoffrey Horton had put through a call to his old friend Antony Maitland on the previous afternoon, for no other reason than to discuss the case.

The sharp sound of the telephone at his elbow seemed to Maitland at the time no more than a minor nuisance. He reached out for the receiver without taking his eyes from the document he was perusing, and said "Uh-huh?" with an inflection of inquiry.

"Are you there?" demanded the telephone in an injured tone.

"Of course I am," said Maitland, still absently. He had recognized the voice, but he hadn't altogether succeeded in disengaging his mind from the matter at hand.

"Are you working?" asked Geoffrey Horton, as though the idea was altogether unreasonable.

"I'm trying to."

"It can't be all that urgent."

"I'm in court on Friday with your revered father-in-law," said Antony, looking up at last and speaking with only a slight exaggeration of patience. "But I've a nasty feeling we're going to get clobbered anyway."

"Then it can't matter if you listen to me for a minute," said Geoffrey, who was nothing if not single-minded.

"I suppose not." He sounded reluctant, but as he pushed the papers away a token six inches, he felt only relief. "What have you got, Geoffrey?"

"A body."

"Dead?"

"Dead and buried. At least, it was."

"You're not going to tell me you've discovered the secret of eternal life?"

"You know perfectly well what I mean."

"Well then . . . who dug it up?"

"The police."

"Where?"

"In a garden at Oakhurst. The owner's a client of mine."

"Did he put it there?"

"The police seem to think . . . it's rather an involved story, Antony."

"Yes, but where do I come in?"

"I want you to come to Brixton with me tomorrow."

"Now, if you'd said you wanted me to go to the Magistrate's Court—"

"That's been taken care of. The arrest was made on Monday."

"I see. Is this client of yours male or female?"

"Male."

"And the deceased?"

"A woman, probably about thirty, so far unidentified."

"Not the one I read about in the paper . . . or rather, didn't read, because the headline '*Faceless Corpse*' rather put me off."

"The same. She'd been strangled," Horton added, as though this might somehow constitute an added inducement.

"How long had she been underground?"

"Two months . . . three months . . . you can never be sure about a thing like that."

"And she hasn't been identified?"

"No."

"But in spite of that, your client has been arrested. It all sounds most unlikely to me."

"There are circumstances—"

"Now we're getting to it."

"Well, no, as a matter of fact. I'd rather you heard the story from Langton himself."

"Is that his name?"

"Dr. Henry Langton. Yes."

"What sort of a doctor?"

"He's the local G.P."

"I suppose the police think he might find a private graveyard useful on occasion."

"This is serious, Antony."

"Did he do it, anyway? Did he strangle this woman . . . whoever she is?"

"He says not, and I believe him. Up to a point."

"Come now, it must be one thing or the other."

"I don't think he killed her, but he's hiding something. I thought perhaps you could tell me what he's lying about."

"My dear Geoffrey, I haven't got second sight. Anyway, if you're working on a Not Guilty plea, are you sure you want to know?"

"I don't want the prosecution to have the chance of springing something on you entirely unforeseen."

"If you're so considerate of my feelings, why not try offering the brief to someone else?" Horton didn't speak, but he hadn't expected an answer, after all. "All right, then, I can manage tomorrow," he added, and grimaced at the document he had been studying. "Shall I meet you there, or will you pick me up?"

Thursday, 20th May

Of all the jobs that raised in Maitland a fierce disinclination, prison visiting was just about the worst. That May morning was no exception; a cool but sunlit morning, when even in London the air seemed sparkling clear . . . an illusion that didn't persist for an instant when they got inside the building, and was altogether forgotten by the time they were incarcerated in the interview room, waiting for their client.

Geoffrey Horton was a solicitor with a lucrative practice that was largely criminal. He had red hair and a disposition that was normally cheerful, but he had been oddly uncommunicative on the way down, and Antony was beginning to be curious. Geoffrey was apt to see things in black and white, without admitting the possibility that they might be a nice shade of gray, and he was very far from being naïve.

Maitland himself had made a mental picture of Dr. Langton—a youngish man, impossibly smooth and polished—to which he had taken a quite unwarrantable dislike; and against all experience, he was surprised when the door opened to admit the reality. So surprised that for once he was not aware of the usual pang of distaste as the door swung shut again with the warder outside; it took him a moment to sort out his impressions at all.

At the second glance he had to admit that though Henry Langton was good-looking, his good looks did not go beyond what was reasonable. The doctor was of middle height; about thirty-five, at a guess; his suit was expensive, but carelessly worn, as though this was of little importance, and the pockets sagged in a way that his tailor must have found distressing. But Antony's predominant thought was "too sensitive by half," and that added another factor to his curiosity. He sat at the end of the long table, watching the newcomer until he was seated too, listening to Horton's words of introduction without really hearing them. Langton was calm . . . too calm. Shake him a little, then? When the solicitor stopped speaking, he said, without much inflection in his tone, "You don't look like the sort of chap to go in for do-it-yourself grave digging."

A slight frown appeared between Langton's eyes. He glanced at Horton, and then back at Maitland again. "I'm not, of course," he said. And then, with a touch of humor, "How did you guess?"

"Before we go into that, you'd better put me in the picture. A woman has been found murdered . . . strangled—"

"There were . . . other injuries," said Langton, as though reluctantly.

"So I gathered."

"Her face had been disfigured. Badly."

"To prevent identification?"

"Enough for that," said Langton, still unwillingly.

"And you are as much in the dark about that as the police are?"

"Yes, but you see—"

"We'd better start at the beginning. Dr. Langton. When, and how, was the discovery made?"

"A neighbor's children, playing hide-and-seek in the shrubbery. They had a dog with them, and it started to dig. As to when, last Saturday . . . five days ago."

"Did they come to you?"

"No, they ran away. Scared to death, poor little devils, I should think. It wasn't until that evening that one of them told his parents. Next thing I knew, the police were on the doorstep."

"How long had she been dead?"

"They didn't go into that at the—the hearing; I daresay the autopsy findings haven't been reported in detail yet. I'd say two months, but I'd be guessing . . . and I do have something to go on, you see."

"What is that?"

"I was away for a week two months ago, and I don't see when else it could have been done."

"And this woman had been strangled. Manually? With a stocking? With a cord?"

"With a cord. It was still around her neck."

"Her clothes?"

"I don't know. I saw her at the graveside . . . the earth was muddy, and it clung to her; she hadn't been cleaned up at all. Afterward, at the mortuary, there was just her face . . . what had been her face. And a birthmark, but they showed me that separately, you see."

"But still you couldn't identify her?"

"No."

"I wonder now . . . what connection do the police suggest between you, other than the fact that she was found on your property?"

"They haven't . . . precisely . . . suggested any connection yet."

"There must be more than that." Maitland's tone had sharpened, and he glanced at Horton as he spoke.

Geoffrey shrugged and said impassively, "The cord used came from a blind on the surgery window, and one of Dr. Langton's handkerchiefs—identified by the laundry mark—was found clutched in her hand. Someone had been into the house, and there were no signs of breaking and entering."

"Any explanation for that?" His eyes were on the doctor again.

"None at all."

"Had you noticed the cord was missing . . . had it been replaced?"

"It's a north window, I rarely use that blind."

"Their case is still so thin as to be practically transparent." He got up and began to move restlessly across the room. "These circumstances you spoke of, Horton . . . they make a difference, I suppose."

"They do." As he still seemed disinclined to speak, Maitland turned to Henry Langton again. "The police have some particular reason, other than you have told me, for looking on you with suspicion."

"I'm afraid that's true."

"You'd better tell me." And now, at last, Langton was shaken out of that unnatural calm.

"It was nothing I did. I had an alibi, an incontrovertible alibi—"

"For what?"

"The murder of my wife."

There was a moment's silence. Maitland's expression could have told him nothing. "Which you did not—of course! —commit," he said after a while, in a flat tone that held no hint of skepticism.

"I told you—"

"Ah, yes, the alibi. You'd better give me the full story, Dr. Langton. I seem to be getting confused."

"It happened a year ago," said Geoffrey unexpectedly.

"More than that," Langton corrected him. "Fifteen—nearly sixteen months."

"I realize this must be distressing for you."

"Not at all!" snapped Langton, with the first hint he had shown of temper. Maitland smiled at him; in a way, the very naturalness of the reaction was reassuring.

"Horton could tell me, of course. But I'd rather hear it from you."

"I was out on a call. Ruth was strangled while I was at my patient's house."

"How was the time so positively established?"

"We were entertaining friends. They stayed perhaps twenty minutes after I had gone. Someone phoned the police about half an hour after that. They investigated, and found her . . . strangled."

"In the same way as the other?"

"In precisely the same way."

"Who telephoned?"

"No one knows; he didn't give his name, and he never came forward." Langton paused (imagination working overtime, thought Antony, suddenly—and to his annoyance—sympathetic). "He said he saw a shadow on the blind."

An ugly picture. "And your patient?" Maitland asked.

"A woman who had lived in the neighborhood not more than a month or two—"

"Six months," said Horton, setting the record straight.

"How long were you out of the house?"

"An hour and a quarter, an hour and twenty minutes. Something like that."

"Rather a lengthy sick call, wouldn't you say?"
"Not really. I had to get the car out, and the drive would take ten minutes or so, I suppose."
"I see."
"But I hardly knew her, they couldn't suggest any connection between us."
"Had you met her socially?"
"Once or twice."
"What was her occupation?"
"I always assumed she had private means."
"You never thought it might have been a put-up job . . . that call?"
Again there was the quick frown, the quick glance at the speaker. "It never occurred to me. Why should it?"
"I don't know. You haven't told us yet that you were framed."
"But I don't think . . . I don't know anyone so spiteful."
"Even now?"
"Even now."
"That brings us to motive. If you didn't kill your wife, how did the murderer get in?"
"She must have let him in herself."
"Someone she knew, then?"
"Not necessarily, in a doctor's house. It was too late to go to the surgery door, but someone with an urgent message—"
"Yes, I see. No servants living in?"
"Only the housekeeper, and she was out that night."
"Her regular time for being off duty?"
"It was."
"Had anything been stolen?"
"Not that I ever discovered. Nothing seemed out of place. No signs of a struggle, even."
"The cord?"
"From the drawing-room window. The room where she was found."
"So at some point she must have left the murderer alone there . . . don't you think?"
"I think she went to fetch the telephone pad from the

hall, to write down a message, perhaps. It was near her, in any case, on the floor . . . the police seemed to think I'd put it there myself."

"Motive, Dr. Langton. Can you think of anyone who had a motive?"

"No one at all. Except myself."

"Had you one?"

"It must have seemed so. Ruth was a semi-invalid, you see, and a wealthy woman. And I did want to marry again; in her condition, I'd never have told her, but—"

"What was wrong?"

"Multiple sclerosis. I know what you're thinking, of course. She might have lived for years. But—I don't know if you can believe this—I still loved her . . . in a way."

"Did you benefit financially from your wife's death?"

"She left me everything."

"I see. Can you suggest any other motive?"

"That's the awful thing. I can't."

"You can take that as true," said Horton, coming out of his silence again. "It was gone into at the time, very thoroughly."

"Did you act for Dr. Langton then?"

"I did."

"I see." This time he drew out the words thoughtfully. "What's worrying you exactly? The prosecution were lucky to get a committal, you know. On the face of it—"

"I think they're hoping to get an identification before the trial comes on."

"How will that help?"

"The witness who provided Dr. Langton's alibi at the time of his wife's death has disappeared."

"That's putting it rather strongly," Langton protested. "She's left the neighborhood—"

"Leaving no forwarding address. She could have broken your alibi, you know, as easily as she originally provided it."

"Easier," said Langton, his voice suddenly hard. And then, faintly apologetic, "The police weren't at all inclined to believe her," he explained.

"If they can obtain an identification—"

"But if it was this—this missing witness," said Maitland, disliking the faintly melodramatic flavor of the phrase, "surely Dr. Langton would know."

"I couldn't recognize her, if that's what you mean. Nobody could."

"No distinguishing marks, other than her features?"

"I told you, I didn't know the woman well."

"As her doctor—"

"She was suffering from fibrositis. I never had occasion to make a thorough examination."

"If we can demonstrate that she is still alive . . . I suppose you're doing something about that, Horton."

"I have it in hand."

"Well, if we can, the other points can be fairly easily dealt with, I think." (Already the phrases were weaving themselves in his mind.)

"Her name was Molly Browne," said Langton abruptly into the silence. "Not exactly uncommon. She was a widow, she said."

"Any reason for disbelieving her?"

"I told you, I hardly knew her."

"So you did." He came back to the table again, and pulled an old envelope out of his pocket and began to scribble on the back. "I shall want a view of the location, Horton. Can you arrange that?"

"I'll telephone Mrs. Langton."

"Mrs.—?" He looked from one of them to the other, and his eyes finally came to rest on the doctor's face. "Oh, I see, you married again."

"I did." Langton smiled as he spoke, but a little wryly. "When I mentioned I was away from home two months ago . . . that was my honeymoon."

"You're still living in the house your wife—your first wife—died in?"

"I hadn't much choice. There's the practice, you see; and even if I could have found a suitable property, it might have seemed like running away."

"Have you met any prejudice?"

"Oddly enough, very little." He paused, and then added in a matter-of-fact tone, "It will be different now, of course."

"We shall have plenty of time later to worry about that," Maitland pointed out. "Meanwhile, Dr. Langton, we will start again at the beginning, and go into everything in just a little more detail."

/ 2 /

Outside in the sunshine again, they walked slowly toward the car. Maitland seemed preoccupied, but Geoffrey was simmering with impatience, and after a while he said curtly, "Tell me, at least, how he impressed you."

Maitland turned his head and gave him a grin, but his tone was serious. "Intensely self-conscious. Too thin-skinned for his own good. I can't think of any reason for his choosing the medical profession, unless he's dedicated to his work as only a few doctors are. I mean, I imagine there are times when it makes him perfectly miserable."

"Not the sort of person, then—"

"I can see him as a mercy murderer . . . I think. If his wife was in pain."

"It isn't her death we have to worry about. Or only"—he corrected himself—"only indirectly."

"The most humane of men can turn into murderers, if the climate is right."

"He couldn't have killed his wife," said Horton, with the air of one advancing an unshakable argument.

"He might have arranged her death. As for what he was lying about, do you want me to guess?"

"Yes, I do."

"That must be the first time . . . we must have a drink to celebrate." Geoffrey waved the suggestion impatiently aside. "However, at a guess, I'd say he knows damn well who the woman is, and when the police find out—"

"That's what I was afraid of," said Horton gloomily. And dropped his key ring as they came up to the car, and swore.

/ 3 /

They lunched together, and talked (a counterirritant) of the very dull case that Maitland was working on. Horton was inclined to be querulous about the suggestion that they should go to Oakhurst that very afternoon, but he agreed at last, and they went out to where he had left the Humber. "It's good for my reputation to be seen with you in this," said Antony, settling himself; and Geoffrey smiled, because the car had been new earlier in the year, and as far as he was concerned, the charm hadn't yet worn off.

Oakhurst, though in the London area, prides itself on being still a village. There is the common, of course, and the bus service tends to be infrequent, and it is practically impossible to live there and be more than a stone's throw away from the nearest public house, so perhaps they have reason. But the lane is now solidly blocked in on both sides by tall apartment buildings, which—though they offer a long list of amenities—are short on beauty, and it cannot be said that they contribute much to the illusion.

Dr. Langton's house, Oak Dene, was large and old-fashioned; so much could be seen from the gate. The lawns in front of the house were trim, and had a cared-for look, but the shrubbery on the right of the drive was thick and gloomy. Maitland stopped and eyed it in a doubtful way. "In there?" he asked.

"There's a path," said Geoffrey, gesticulating. "All the same, it isn't the most cheerful place on earth."

"Spiders," said Antony, finding the path and starting down it. "And black beetles down the back of your neck, I shouldn't wonder."

"Well, you would come."

"The call of duty. Where . . . oh, here we are." He halted, and Horton came up beside him. The bushes were thinner here, and there was a high brick wall ahead, the sort of wall that issues a mute, irresistible challenge to any proper boy. They were quite out of sight of the house again, and at their feet was a roughly dug hole, unpleasantly suggestive in shape, with earth piled untidily beyond.

"A pleasant playground," a deep voice remarked unexpectedly, and with more than a hint of irony. Maitland jumped.

"Oh, it's you, Chief Inspector," he said reproachfully, and turned his attention again to the shallow grave. "A sort of horrid attraction . . . is that what you mean?"

"Something like that."

"You know each other, don't you? Yes, of course you do. You didn't tell me, Geoffrey, that this was one of Chief Inspector Sykes's affairs."

"I didn't know."

The detective was a square-built man, with dark hair just beginning to streak with gray, a voice that still gave evidence of his north-country origin, and a placid disposition. "Well, now," he said, smiling in a sedate way from one of them to the other, "it isn't rightly my business. I was curious, you see."

"Were you, though?" Antony gave him rather a blank look. "I suppose you know the prosecution haven't got a leg to stand on."

"Would you say that?" Sykes seemed to consider the point. "Well, I won't say Inspector Conway didn't act a bit overzealous like; but there, you'll not be blaming a man for that."

"He was inspired, I suppose?" inquired Maitland sarcastically. He was not fond of Inspector Conway.

"Something like that. With the pointers we've got—"

"Her clothes? What about them?"

"A wool dress. Red, it had been . . . cheerful," said Sykes with a note of regret. "No coat or hat or gloves or handbag, and it must have been cold when she was killed."

"That's something we'll never know for sure," said Maitland positively.

"I wouldn't say that. For instance, it was on a Tuesday—"

"How do you know?"

"It was embroidered on her panties . . . briefs, I suppose you'd call them," said Sykes, so solemnly that it was several seconds before Maitland, startled, realized that he had perpetrated a pun. "Inspector Conway tells me some of the stores sell them . . . one pair for every day of the week."

"It might have been her name," said Antony perversely. "Or she might have been born on a Tuesday and been proud of it . . . 'Tuesday's child is full of grace' . . . you know."

"I'm sorry to throw cold water on all your suggestions, but I don't think you can buy them, not except in sets," said Sykes, still earnestly. And then, without any change of tone, "You wouldn't be getting any ideas about this case, would you, Mr. Maitland?"

"If I were, you're the last person I should confide in, Chief Inspector."

"I daresay. But seeing you here like this—"

"It isn't unusual to view the terrain."

"No, but I shouldn't like Inspector Conway to get nervous," said Sykes. Maitland smiled at him, but this time there was no amusement behind the smile.

"I can't say that worries me unduly. In fact, I shall look forward to seeing him in court."

"Now, Mr. Maitland—"

"Well, Chief Inspector?"

Sykes glanced at Geoffrey Horton, and then looked back at Maitland again: a tall man with a casual air, and something that was not at all casual in his eyes just then. "Mr. Horton's an old friend, so perhaps it won't matter if what I'm going to say is indiscreet."

"I don't believe you were ever indiscreet in your life."

"Be that as it may, you may think that what I'm going to say—" He broke off, and started again, rephrasing the sentence. "Does it occur to you, Mr. Maitland, that because your own experience with the police has not been—shall we say?—uniformly happy—"

"You may say so, but it's the understatement of the year."

"—it does not follow that we shall always be in the wrong?" He saw Maitland's expression harden, and shook his head at him gently. "Think it over," he advised.

"You're saying I'm prejudiced. I am, of course. You can leave this present business out of it, because I don't know anything about it . . . yet. But the idea that you people are always right—"

"Nay, now, I didn't say that," Sykes protested, hurt. "I just don't want you to get embittered, that's all."

"It's qu-quite enough," said Maitland, and pulled himself up on the edge of anger. He thrust his hands in his pockets, and began to look around him in a deliberate way. "You were quite right, Geoffrey. There's nothing to see. Except that it's not very deep. And that being so . . . was the birthmark really all that well preserved?"

"It was on the sole of her foot; I suppose her shoes afforded some protection," said Horton. "In any case, it's quite identifiable." But he added, to Sykes, "If you can get anyone to identify it, of course."

"It's early days yet," said the detective in his placid way. "Well, I've seen what I wanted, and like you, I'm not much wiser, so I'll bid you gentlemen good day."

"We're going too," Maitland told him. They went in single file along the narrow path to the drive, where Sykes turned toward the gate. For the first time it occurred to Antony that there had not been a police car anywhere in sight.

"He was right, you know," said Geoffrey, as they walked toward the house.

"Don't you start! It was your idea, after all."

"I know. I only mean—"

"I have a great regard for the police," said Maitland. "As a matter of fact."

"For some of them," Horton corrected him precisely.

"You seem to be suggesting that I may turn into the sort of chap who automatically claims his client has been beaten up to get a confession; and that probably there's been evidence planted as well."

"No, I—"

"Sykes knows better than that."

"All the same," said Geoffrey, struggling doggedly on to

the end of his sentence, "it wouldn't do your—your professional image any good to get that sort of a reputation."

"Whose idea was it—?"

"Mine, of course. It doesn't invalidate what I've been saying," said Horton, and reached the door and pressed the bell, not unthankfully. Then he turned and smiled at his companion. "After all, you have to start again somewhere."

"I wasn't aware I'd ever stopped."

"It's your first murder case since—" The door opened, and he turned and went on, almost without a break, "I was wondering . . . oh, good morning, Mrs. Langton. I'm sorry to trouble you, but can you spare us a few minutes?"

"Yes, of course."

"This is Mr. Maitland." He stepped into the hall, and Antony followed him, not really listening to the introduction, but watching the girl who had opened the door. She was tall—his first impression was that she was almost as tall as her husband—and her dark hair was soft and shining, and she was paler than anyone had a right to be. There were no traces of tears, but when she spoke, her voice had a husky quality that might or might not be natural.

"We'll go into the drawing room, shall we? It isn't very tidy, I'm afraid. I've been using it as a workroom." There was a long table under the windows, with a sewing machine and a pile of flowered material. The rest of the room was tidy enough, a little lifeless even. She sat down on the edge of one of the chairs near the fireplace and clasped her hands around her knees. How old was she . . . twenty-two . . . twenty-three? It occurred to Maitland that perhaps she had forgotten how to relax.

"We saw your husband this morning," Horton was saying, as he, in turn seated himself. "He seemed well, I thought." She inclined her head, the only sign that she had heard him. "Now, there are one or two questions—?"

"More than that," said Maitland, interrupting him. "We'd better get that clear from the beginning." He paused a moment, looking around the room. "Aren't you lonely here?"

"In a way, of course. There's plenty to do." Her eyes

followed his to the pile of sewing. "Not that. That's not important. But Ian Bannister—my husband's assistant—someone's got to look after him."

"The housekeeper?" said Geoffrey.

"She left. I'm glad, really. She didn't think . . . she thought Henry . . . well, anyway, I'm glad. Ian is staying at the Angel . . . that would be just one more scandal, wouldn't it, if we were here together? But he's terribly busy, of course, and he can't manage regular meals, and I don't at all mind being alone at night."

Antony thought the speech was not unrehearsed; some solicitous relative, perhaps. He was filled with the urge to prowl around the room as he put his questions, but she might find the movement disturbing. He compromised by sitting down on the arm of the sofa. "Shall we go straight to the heart of the matter, Mrs. Langton? It's a question of deciding whether we shall call you as a witness, you see. So I want you to tell me about your relations with your husband, while his first wife was still alive."

She flushed then. "I don't . . . there was never—" Her voice was steady, though her speech was broken. What had Geoffrey said her name was . . . Susan? An old-fashioned touch; perhaps it suited her. "I don't see," she added more firmly, "what it has to do with you."

"You're going to have to take my word for that, Mrs. Langton. I hope you will."

"Very well, then. We saw quite a lot of each other. I knew he liked me, sometimes I was almost sure he loved me. But there was Ruth, you see."

"That made a difference?"

"I'm trying to be honest. It's easy to say you wouldn't do anything to hurt someone, but I don't know if I'd have thought about that if she hadn't been so nice."

"Dr. Langton never spoke to you of the possibility of marriage at some future date?"

"No. Oh, no!"

"Or of some—I suppose I must say some improper relationship during her lifetime?"

"No."

"Was anything said between you that might have been misunderstood?"

"I don't—I don't think so. I ought to tell you, though, some of my friends seemed to guess. About my feelings, I mean. And when we were engaged, my mother said, 'I wondered how long you were going to wait.' I don't know . . . it's so difficult to know . . . what everyone really thought."

"But as far as you and Dr. Langton were concerned, there was never any discussion of the future?"

"Not until after Ruth died. Six months after, to be exact. I know Henry was trying to do the right thing."

"I see. Did you know Mrs. Browne?"

This time she didn't answer straight away. "Mr. Maitland, you say you're trying to help us—"

Geoffrey had said that, hadn't he? Something like that. "Will you leave it to me for the present . . . what's important, and what isn't?"

"I suppose I must, but I don't understand," she said helplessly.

"Never mind." He smiled at her. "That makes two of us." She did not return his smile, but to his surprise she went back to the question without prompting.

"Molly Browne. I met her several times at the houses of friends."

"Not an intimate acquaintance?"

"No. Quite casual."

"When did she leave Oakhurst?"

"I don't remember exactly. Sometime in the spring."

"Last spring?"

"Yes. I remember Mrs. Harper saying that she'd been to say good-bye. She was going back to her own home . . . something like that."

"Dr. Langton has told us that he believes she had private means. Do you remember anything that would confirm that, or contradict it?"

"Mrs. Harper might know. I think—I'm sure sometimes I used to see her during the week, so she couldn't have had an ordinary job."

"Did you like her?"

"Yes, I did. She was friendly, and full of life." She hesitated, biting her lip. "Do you think it was Molly who—who was found?"

"An unknown woman," Maitland told her. "There's been no identification yet."

"Then why are you asking me all these questions?"

"Because—like you—I'm wondering." He got up as he spoke, and walked to the window and back. "Did Dr. Langton—?"

"Henry never said a word. Only what you have done . . . an unknown woman."

"When she was found, do *you* think he knew who it was?"

"I'm sure—I'm sure he didn't. He was upset when he saw her, but it wasn't like an ordinary death, you know. And he couldn't have had anything to do with it, whatever they say, because I should have known."

"When were you married?"

"On the twenty-seventh of February. We were away for a week, and Mrs. Jackson—the housekeeper—was away for five days at the same time, and Ian Bannister went to the Angel, and the *locum* stayed there too, and I know it was frightfully inconvenient, which is why—" She broke off, spreading her hands. "You aren't interested in that. I was trying to tell you it must have been then."

"You don't think anyone could have dug a grave in the shrubbery without your knowledge?"

"Well, could they? I know it's very cut off from the house, and the children come over the wall and play there, and we never know unless one of us happens to be going down the drive, and even then we don't mind, of course. The thing is, nobody would feel safe when the house was occupied; doctors are in and out at all hours. That applies to Henry, too . . . Ian might have caught him. But when everybody was away—"

"It's a good point, Mrs. Langton. Did Dr. Bannister attend Mrs. Ruth Langton, do you know?"

"No, that was Dr. Fielding. He was her family's doctor, long before she was married."

"I see. When you came home from your honeymoon, was there anything to suggest what might have happened during your absence?"

"Well, no. But it was the first time I'd lived here, you see, I might not have noticed. Mother thought it was dreadful, our coming back here, but . . . a doctor's house, you know. Henry said I could change anything I wanted; that's what I've been trying to get on with, I can't stand these blue curtains, and it's something to do. I wanted to change the garden, too, the shrubbery is ghastly, and if he'd agreed, it might have been better, because then it would have been us who found her—people working for us, I mean—and they couldn't have said we were hiding anything."

"Dr. Langton didn't care for the idea?" asked Maitland, disentangling this without too much difficulty.

"I don't suppose he felt as I did about it; he was born here," she told him. "And I'm sure he'd have agreed in the long run, but it's too late to think about that now. Mr. Maitland, do you think . . . they couldn't possibly find him guilty, could they? Mr. Horton said 'don't worry'"—she turned her head and gave Geoffrey a rather wavering smile—"but I don't know whether he was just being kind."

The implications of this might have disturbed Maitland's gravity, if he hadn't felt at the same time that the situation was very far from amusing. "On the evidence as it stands," he said carefully, "we should get a verdict."

"But that isn't enough! It would just mean they couldn't prove it, and everyone would still think Henry did it. But you said 'on the evidence,' didn't you? Does that mean you think it was Molly Browne who was killed?"

"It means I very much hope that Molly Browne can be traced, and will turn up alive and well. You'd already thought of the possibility, hadn't you, Mrs. Langton?"

"There was so much talk when Ruth died, and even when Molly said where he had been, there were still some people who said 'where there's smoke' . . . things like that. So I know what it would mean."

"I see."

"But how can anyone identify her? Henry said—"

"There are several ways. Dental work, for instance. A birthmark."

"Who would know a thing like that? She lived alone, she never spoke of any family. And her husband was dead."

"We must wait and see." He got up then, and stood looking down at her. "Wouldn't your mother come and stay?"

"I don't want . . . I'd rather be alone."

She really was extraordinarily goodlooking, he thought, even with that unnatural pallor. And for this reason—and others—it will be better not to call her as a witness. "What was Mrs. Ruth Langton like?" he asked rather abruptly, following this train of thought.

"She was . . . I'll show you." She went over to an old-fashioned bureau and pulled open one of the drawers. "Henry put it away, I felt rather guilty about that. As though you could somehow hurt a person by denying their memory." She crossed the room again and thrust the framed photograph into Maitland's hands. "There you are," she said.

A wedding picture. Henry Langton, younger, smiling; the bride, a small, fair girl with a gentle expression. Not much character, perhaps, or was that one of the things you couldn't tell? He said, "Thank you," because he couldn't think of any comment that would be appropriate, and handed the photograph to Geoffrey, leaving him with the problem of its disposal. And all of a sudden he was urgent to be gone.

"Mr. Horton will be in touch with you, Mrs. Langton, but if I can help you in any way—" True enough, but no sense saying it. . . . "One last question: I suppose Dr. Bannister takes some time off each week?"

"Yes, of course. They take alternate weekends, so far as can be arranged; and then he has Tuesday each week."

"And the housekeeper, Mrs. Jackson?"

"Wednesdays and Sundays. Always."

"I see. Then I needn't worry you any more, Mrs. Langton." Maitland began to move toward the door. Geoffrey stooped and put the photograph face downward on the coffee table. It would go back into the drawer, of course; there was nothing else to be done with it.

She came with them to the top of the steps, and when Antony turned at the corner of the drive, she was still standing there, staring after them. He took away with him an impression of stillness.

/ 4 /

He had told Jenny before he left that morning about the visit to Brixton, and she had said, "What a bore for you, Antony," just as if she didn't know how he really felt about it. A foolish pretense which, perhaps equally foolishly, he found comforting. Now, when he got home, there was a heartening smell of stew, and the fire had been lighted against his coming, and the big living room had taken on the air of untroubled tranquillity with which his wife surrounded herself . . . whenever outside influences would permit.

The house in Kempenfeldt Square was formed nominally of two establishments, Sir Nicholas Harding, its owner, occupying its two main floors, while the Maitlands had their quarters above. It was an arrangement of long standing, and they all seemed to have forgotten now that once it had been regarded as temporary; and though a few of the original self-imposed restrictions still remained, they had mainly fallen into disuse. Maitland was in his uncle's chambers, and the convenience of a joint establishment was undeniable, though it had its drawbacks too, as he would have been the first to point out.

That evening when he got in, Sir Nicholas and Jenny were sitting in a companionable silence, Jenny in her favorite corner of the sofa, Sir Nicholas in the wing chair that was almost invariably devoted to his use. Antony saw that both their glasses were filled, helped himself to sherry, and came across to stand with his back to the fire. "I didn't know you were honoring us with your company tonight, Uncle Nick."

"A domestic crisis," said Sir Nicholas, with all the serenity of a man who has found a safe refuge. He was as tall as his nephew, though rather more heavily built, with fair hair and an authoritative manner of which he was quite unconscious. "Some trouble with the electric range," he went on. "It was explained to me at length, but I really cannot remember exactly what it was." He sipped his sherry. "You're late, Antony. I thought you told me you were well ahead with that case of Bellerby's."

"That was yesterday. It's hopeless, anyway. There's nothing I, or anybody else, can do."

"What's so bad about it?" Jenny asked. "I admit it doesn't sound really exciting."

"Excitement, my dear, is the last thing one should aim at," Sir Nicholas told her, but he was watching his nephew as he spoke. "It is a nice, straightforward affair concerning the transfer of property—"

"That's just what I'm complaining of. That it's so obvious, I mean. Our client is making his claim as a matter of principle, he says, but I can't see that he has the faintest case in equity."

"I don't suppose he cares about that," said Jenny, "so long as he feels he's in the right."

"Perhaps not." He was unwilling to relinquish his grievance. "What am I supposed to tell the court, anyway? 'My client will inform you that the land in question is nobbut space out o' doors, and therefore not worth arguing over.' He doesn't seem to see that makes his whole attitude unreasonable."

"Perhaps he murdered his grandmother and buried her under the fifth gorse bush," Jenny suggested idly; but then she looked more closely at her husband. "That isn't Geoffrey's case, is it? The one with the faceless corpse?"

"The very same."

"Did you read about it, Uncle Nick? Somebody buried a body in a doctor's garden at Oakhurst—"

"I never read the more sensational items in my newspaper," said Sir Nicholas dampeningly.

"No, but this sounded interesting. They arrested the

doctor, which seems a shame, because he'd only just got married."

"Illogical, love." Antony looked down at her with affection.

"Well, did he do it?"

"My instructions are that he didn't."

"Yes, but what do you think?"

"I haven't the faintest idea." That was true, wasn't it . . . or almost true? "Anyway, as it stands, we've a good chance of getting an acquittal."

"As it stands," Sir Nicholas repeated inquiringly.

"Oh, well, you never know, after all. There are two counts against him: if his wife—his new wife—is telling the truth, he was unduly cautious in the length of time he allowed to elapse after his first wife's death before he approached her."

"What has that to do with the body of an unknown woman?"

Antony told him.

"Tenuous," said Sir Nicholas severely. "*And* complicated."

"The other thing is simpler. It's just that he wouldn't let Susan have the shrubbery uprooted, though he gave her *carte blanche* to make what alterations she wanted to the house. He implied that it was a matter of sentiment, which I doubt; but as the jury will have no cognizance of either point, I don't propose to worry my head about them."

To his relief, Sir Nicholas did not pursue the matter just then. He wasn't quite sure why he didn't want to discuss the other possible complications, but he was certain at least that he had no intention of telling his uncle about the brief encounter with Chief Inspector Sykes.

Part Two

Trinity Term, 1965

Monday, 21st June

The recess came and went, and the Trinity term began. Maitland was in Sir Nicholas' room in chambers, arguing halfheartedly about a writ *Ne exeat regno*, when Geoffrey Horton phoned to give him the news. "The Langton case," he said. "I told you this was going to happen. A woman named Armstrong has identified the dead girl as her daughter, Mary."

"Her married daughter?"

"She doesn't know. The girl left home nearly four years ago. The thing is, however, that Mary Armstrong's photograph has been identified in Oakhurst as being one of Molly Browne."

"That's torn it."

"A speaking likeness," quoted Geoffrey gloomily. "What have you got to say to that?"

"It means—oh, lord!—I suppose it means he did it," said Antony. He found the thought depressed him. "There wasn't much question of a mercy murder about Molly Browne's death, was there?"

"That's not all. The prosecution—"

"You don't have to tell me. *No rule of practice shall prevent both murders being charged in the same indictment.* We shall have a fight on our hands, that's all. What does Langton have to say for himself?"

"He wants to see you."

"Yes, I suppose he does. You don't imagine he's going to give us the old tale about finding her dead, do you?"

"He hasn't said that . . . so far," said Geoffrey cautiously.

"Well, there's no desperate hurry about it. Fix it up for the end of the week, if you can." He turned from the telephone a few moments later and gave his uncle a look eloquent of despair.

"The doctor?" asked Sir Nicholas.

"It is." He repeated what Geoffrey had told him. "He'll stick to the Not Guilty plea, of course, but the coincidence is too big for any jury to swallow."

"Too big even for you?"

"I'm afraid so." He got up and walked to the window, and Sir Nicholas' eyes followed him with a look that was faintly amused. "He's the sort who makes his own hell," said Antony after a moment. "It's hard to judge a chap like that."

"The departure from normal standards of conduct seems a little drastic," said Sir Nicholas in his mildest tone; at which Antony grinned, and came back to the desk again.

/ 2 /

Sykes called him the same evening. "You've heard the news about your friend, Dr. Langton?" he inquired.

"I have."

"I thought you might like to know that Mrs. Armstrong has a daughter."

"Mary Armstrong, alias Molly Browne."

"Another daughter, Kathleen. The prosecution have no use for her, so if you want to find out anything about the family background—"

"It's kind of you, Chief Inspector, but unless she knows something about her sister's death, she's no use to me."

"You're slipping, Mr. Maitland." There was no doubt about the amusement in Sykes's voice now.

Antony said seriously, "Let's just say I was willing to heed the voice of reason when you spoke to me the other day." He heard the Chief Inspector's deep chuckle at the other end of the wire, and held the receiver farther away from his ear.

Friday, 25th June

After the weeks in prison, Henry Langton was looking definitely haggard, but he still covered any tension he might be feeling with an air of deliberate calm. "I want to tell you everything that happened," he said.

Maitland did not look up from the sketch he had started on the back of an old envelope. "I suppose Mr. Horton has explained the position."

"That if I tell you the truth, you've got to act on it. Yes, he has."

"I should not be in a position to put forward a defense I knew to be a lie," said Maitland, as though he had not heard. "If you understand that—"

"I do."

"Then, go ahead." He looked up, and found Langton's eyes fixed on him, and smiled faintly and put down his pencil. "Go ahead," he repeated.

"It's about Molly Browne. I really was at her house the night Ruth was killed, you know."

"But not, perhaps, at the times you stated," said Maitland helpfully. Henry Langton gaped at him.

"What do you mean? The thing is, you see, nobody else knew, or was in a position to know, where I was. I took the message myself, and her cottage was at the end of a lane—"

"You're telling me that now she is known to be dead, you have no alibi for the time your wife was killed."

"Of course I haven't. I do wish you'd let me tell this my own way. Molly Browne phoned me because she had what turned out to be an acute case of fibrositis . . . couldn't put her foot to the ground. I went, of course, knowing she was alone, and prescribed, and told her I would arrange for someone to bring the things out to her the next day. Then she asked me if I would like some coffee. I shouldn't have agreed in the ordinary way, but as she was almost helpless, I thought she might want some herself, so I stayed, and made it, and drank a cup before I left."

"That's all quite clear." He hadn't the faintest idea why Langton was going into all this, but if it made him any happier . . .

"It isn't important, but it explains why I was so long . . . you raised that point, I remember. The important thing is what happened next day. She telephoned me—this woman, Molly Browne—and said she must see me. She said she didn't want to tell the police anything that contradicted my story. I told her, of course, that all she had to do was tell the truth, and she said, 'Truth is relative,' and somehow I didn't like the sound of that, so I picked up the prescriptions and went out to Rose Cottage myself."

"And then—" prompted Maitland, when the pause lengthened. For the first time, Henry seemed to be hesitating, picking his words.

"This is the part you may find hard to believe," he said at last. "She was walking quite normally when I got there, and she laughed and said I'd effected a miraculous cure. Then she told me she wanted five thousand pounds to confirm my alibi to the police."

"She . . . what?"

"She wanted five thousand pounds—"

"I heard you the first time. Are you seriously telling me that the whole thing had been arranged with a view to blackmailing you."

"What else is there to think?"

"You realize that if the sick call was a fake, it follows that she knew what was going to happen to Ruth, that the whole thing had been rigged with some third party, that . . . oh, I give it up."

"I'm telling you exactly that. I don't see how else it could have been."

"Glory be!" said Maitland, and sat for a moment staring. "I don't know about you, Geoffrey," he added, without turning his head, "but this is worse than I imagined."

"I'm telling you the truth," Langton protested.

"Are you though? Do you realize how it would sound in court . . . if I were fool enough to put it to the jury? You killed your wife, and paid—I suppose you did pay?—for an alibi."

"Yes, I paid."

"Or, if you actually persuaded the jury that you'd been to Rose Cottage, the obvious corollary is that you paid for the murder, and got the alibi thrown in as a sort of make-weight."

"But that isn't true."

"It's what they'll believe. Hadn't you better think again?"

"I can't help it," said Langton, doggedly now. "I said I wanted to tell you what happened, and I have."

"She got you out with a trumped-up story of—what did you say?—fibrositis—"

"That's right, it's very painful."

"—kept you there while you made coffee . . . I suppose you're quite sure that at that stage she wasn't making a pass at you."

"Quite sure."

"Because if the blackmail was spur-of-the-moment, it would be easier to believe. She did all this while her partner was back in Oakhurst, murdering your wife, and then calmly asked you for five thousand quid the next day, and you gave it to her."

"Yes."

"Heaven and earth!" said Maitland, and got to his feet. The room did not offer much scope for his restlessness, but he did the best he could, backward and forward across its width. "It's so stupid I might even end up believing it myself."

"*You* might," said Geoffrey gloomily. "No jury on earth would swallow it. While, as for the judge—"

"Whose list is it on?"

"Conroy's."

"That's right, we can't risk it. Look here, Langton, we can't use this. Are you sure you wouldn't like—"

"To change it for a better story? I haven't a very inventive mind, I'm afraid."

"That isn't what I meant. You needn't necessarily tell me the truth, but don't, for heaven's sake, complicate matters with all this—this—"

"Twaddle," said Geoffrey, with rather less than his usual propriety, seeing counsel for once at a loss for words.

"I can't help it," said Langton slowly, "if you don't believe me."

Maitland came back to the table again. "Did you think it would help matters?" he asked.

"No. I don't know. I thought perhaps . . . there are such things as private detectives, aren't there? I thought perhaps you might be able to find out who—" He broke off and shrugged. "I can't make you believe me," he said.

"Tell me, then: how did Molly Browne—and her partner, I suppose—know of the situation that existed between you and your wife?"

"There was no secret about Ruth's condition . . . I mean, anyone could tell she was ill. And I don't suppose the gossips were slow to draw the correct conclusions."

"Once she was there . . . all right. Why did she come to Oakhurst?"

"I see what you mean, of course. I don't know."

"Was your wife's inheritance of recent date? I'm wondering, you see, if there could have been a story in the press."

"Nothing like that. Her father died when she was a child, and even when she was twenty-one . . . I said she was wealthy, but it wasn't the sort of fortune to excite the newspapers, I'm afraid."

"Then I don't see . . . you say you paid the five thousand. What next?"

"Nothing . . . until the police showed me her body."

"You knew who it was. What identified her? The clothes?"

"No, they looked . . . just colorless rags. It was at the mortuary . . . the birthmark."

"On the sole of her left foot, wasn't it? A mark like a diamond, with one rounded end. So when you told me you didn't examine her, that was just a prevarication."

"I said I didn't make a thorough examination. I looked at her foot, of course. That was where she had . . . she said she had the pain."

"I see. So you lied to the police, and to your solicitor, and to me."

"What would you have done?" When there was no reply, he added, with a sort of impatience, "I'd been married just over two months. I was happy, really happy, for the first time in years. I couldn't . . . oh, well!"

"Tell me about Molly Browne. What was she like?"

"Fair, rather plump, lighthearted . . . nice. I should think everyone liked her. And the queer thing is, even when she told me what she wanted, I still couldn't see around it to the viciousness that must lie behind."

"What about her background?"

"That's more difficult. She told me she was a widow, she seemed in easy circumstances, but she never talked about the past. I don't mean that struck me at the time; the occasion just didn't arise. But Susan knew her better, and she didn't seem to know anything about her either."

"Nobody from the past. Who did she know in Oakhurst, then?"

"I met her at the Harpers'. I had the impression she got about quite a lot."

"How often had you visited Rose Cottage?"

"That was the first time. She'd been to the surgery once or twice before, something trifling. A sore throat, something like that. Ian Bannister could tell you."

Maitland moved restlessly, but seemed to decide against resuming his pacing. Instead, he gripped the back of the chair in front of him, as though it would provide a reliable anchor, and said, spacing the words, "It amounts to this: Molly Browne was part of a conspiracy to murder your wife. The motive for this . . . are you sure there was no one with a grudge against her, against you?"

"That wouldn't be a grudge, it would be an insane hatred."

"Whatever you like to call it."

"As sure as one can be . . . yes."

"The motive, then, was to put you in a position in which you could be blackmailed. Is it correct to say that Rose Cottage is in an out-of-the-way place, where your car would be unlikely to be noticed—"

"The lane is a dead end."

"—so that you would have to rely on Molly Browne's word alone?"

"Yes, that's quite correct."

"And you paid up without a murmur?"

"Hardly that."

"At least, you paid. Didn't you know you were asking for trouble, opening the door to further demands?"

"I know . . . I was afraid. But what else could I do? There'd been talk, you know . . . for all my care there'd been talk about Susan and me. And I'd already told the police where I'd been. If Molly Browne had denied it . . . can't you see?"

"And she told you, I suppose, that it was the last time?"

"I didn't really believe that, but after six months . . . I couldn't wait any longer to talk to Susan. And I thought, if we wait a full year it will be long enough . . . they'd have shown their hand by then."

"What would you have done if you had received another demand?"

"I don't know. I told myself I wouldn't pay again, but I don't know . . . there was Susan, you see."

"How did you pay the five thousand?"

"In cash. It just about cleaned me out, but of course, once probate went through—"

"You were nicely in pocket?"

"I didn't want Ruth's money." He moved his shoulders again, rather as though he were shrugging away a burden. "I suppose that's as hard to believe as all the rest."

"Quite as hard." Something in his tone made Langton look up quickly. For a moment he was acutely aware of his counsel, as if he were seeing him for the first time; there was an alertness about Maitland just then that belied his casual manner; his eyes were amused and friendly, but his hands were clenched tightly on the back of the chair. "Just one other thing," he said. "You told us you were entertaining the night your wife was killed."

"What of it?"

"I should like the names of your friends."

"We were playing bridge. There was Mrs. Harper—"

"The same one who befriended Molly Browne?"

"The same." He smiled, as if at some thought, so that for a moment he looked younger and less strained. "You won't . . . oh, well, you'll see for yourself. The other was my assistant, Ian Bannister."

"What about the shrubbery? Why wouldn't you let Mrs. Langton have it uprooted?"

"Sentiment, I suppose. I also suppose I should have let her have her own way with it, in time."

"I see." He stood a moment, letting the silence lengthen, and then said, without turning his head, "Am I making a fool of myself, Geoffrey? If there's no help for it, we shall just have to investigate on the lines Dr. Langton has indicated . . . that's all."

/ 2 /

Horton made a strangled sound, halfway between resignation and protest, but it was not until they were outside the prison again that he spoke his mind. "It's all very well, you deciding the fellow's innocent; I'm glad of that, of course—"

"It will add a certain something to my advocacy," Maitland agreed thoughtfully. And added, with intent to annoy, "Or would, if I was sure."

"—but to follow a line that you admit yourself will only get our client involved in a charge of conspiracy isn't my idea of being helpful," Geoffrey concluded, rightly ignoring the provocation.

"I see your point," said Antony sympathetically. "We shall have to take the matter a stage further, that's all."

"What do you mean?"

"Someone killed them." He spread his hands in an expansive gesture. "Find out who it was, and we're home and dry. And to that end, my dear Geoffrey," he added quickly, seeing from his companion's expression that he was about to argue the point, "the first thing we need is the address of Miss Kathleen Armstrong."

"I don't see what good that will do you," Horton complained.

Maitland wasn't too sure about that himself, but he only said meekly, "It makes a start." There was no point in arguing; he knew quite well that Geoffrey would let him have his way.

Monday, 28th June

That evening he told Jenny, "She came into chambers like a leaf blown by the wind," and Jenny—whose brown curls were apt to look fairly windswept themselves at times, though her feet generally remained firmly on the ground—laughed at him and said, "How poetic!" and then, "Is she very pretty?"

Antony thought about that for a moment. "Not really," he said at last. "In fact, she looks more like a boy than most boys do nowadays. But there's something about her"—he gestured—"as if she were lost and drifting. I can't explain it any better than that."

If his impression was right it was as well that Geoffrey Horton had her firmly in tow. He brought her into Maitland's room, which was an awkward shape, being long and narrow and rather dark, and maneuvered her into the chair nearest the desk. She gave Maitland a sweet, vague smile when the introductions were made and said, but not as though it mattered, "Catherine, not Kathleen. People call me Cathie."

He wondered how old she was. Younger than Susan Langton, he thought; certainly not more than twenty, perhaps several years younger than that. She wasn't very tall, and her fair, straight hair was cut short . . . not quite a crop, but nearly. Her complexion was clear, without much color, and her eyes were a misty blue . . . perhaps she was short-sighted. Her manner was quiet, but without any suggestion of diffidence.

"I have a snap of Molly here," she said, breaking a silence during which she had studied Maitland with a good deal more candor than he had shown in making his observations. "Mr. Horton said you would like to see it."

"Thank you." Molly Browne was more obviously pretty than her sister. What had Henry Langton said? *Fair, plump, lighthearted . . . rather nice.* There was a frankly exuberant attraction about her that the description didn't catch at all. "May I keep this? Mr. Horton may need it." He put it down on the desk, and raised his eyes just in time to catch a rather jerky nod.

"It's the only one there is," said Cathie, "barring the photo Mum gave to the police. Not that we ever liked that one, it was soulful, sort of; a bit stuck-up. She kept it in a drawer."

"We'll take great care of this one. I'm sorry about your sister, Miss Armstrong. I'm sorry we had to meet under these sad circumstances."

Her head went on one side a little, she seemed to be considering what he had said. "I haven't seen Molly for four years," she told him. "It was awful, knowing what happened to her, but still more awful not knowing, in a way."

"Is that what she was called at home . . . Molly?"

"Everyone except Mother. It suited her, you see. Mary is more cold, don't you think so? Molly wasn't like that."

"No." His eyes went back to the snapshot again. "Was she very popular?"

"Oh, yes! Everyone loved her. I did," she added in a matter-of-fact voice, as though her own feelings were the last thing that should give anyone any concern. "That's why it was so awful when she went away."

"Where did she go?"

"We never knew. She didn't say a word. Just came home one day while I was at school and Mum had gone to the sales, and packed her things and went. Her toilet things, that is, and her newest clothes. I had to wear the others up, which was dreadful, because they didn't really fit very well, and they weren't my style at all."

"Are you still at school?"

"Of course not. That was my last year." Again she paused, perhaps calculating the advisability of the confidence. "I'm nearly twenty-two."

"Do you have a job, Miss Armstrong?"

"I'm in the typing pool at Gridley's. It isn't bad, as jobs go, and I don't have any fares to pay."

"That is near your home in . . . Streatham, isn't it?"

"That's right."

"The same house that your sister left four years ago?"

"Yes, it is. We've lived there all my life. It's a bit big for us now, Mum and me, since Dad died."

"Why did your sister leave?"

"I haven't any idea. If you're thinking there was trouble, well, there were arguments, of course, and Mum isn't one to stand any sauce. But nothing to make her go away, nothing serious. Really."

"You must have had some idea, though, some theory."

"She wasn't having a baby, if that's what you're thinking. She'd have told me that."

"Perhaps she left to get married."

"Why should she? There was nothing to stop her, she was turned twenty-five."

"To save argument—"

"Well . . . perhaps," she admitted grudgingly.

"Was there anyone she might have gone to?"

"We asked everyone we could think of at the time. I don't think there was anyone who would have lied to Mum."

"Any place she seemed specially fond of? It might mean she'd made friends there."

"I don't . . . she always enjoyed her holidays. The Lake District, perhaps . . . but she hadn't been back there for years. Or Brightsea. I don't really know."

"You know she was using the name Browne in Oakhurst. Do you know anyone of that name?"

"Nobody but the grocer. She didn't run off with him."

"But she had lots of friends . . . boyfriends?"

"Dozens!" Cathie admitted cheerfully.

"Anyone in particular?"

"Well—"

"Please try to think."

"I don't see what good it will do you . . . all this."

"We have to try."

"And if you're just out to help the man that killed her—"

"Please! Miss Armstrong!" That was Geoffrey, roused to protest. "You don't know that Dr. Langton is guilty."

"The police think he is," she retorted, "and Mum's giving evidence for them."

He let that one go by. "You wouldn't want an innocent man to be punished, for want of a word from you."

"They'll hang him, won't they?" She sounded as if she was discussing an event of some social interest, no more. "There was an article I read in the paper about multiple murders, naming no names, but it was easy to see what they meant." There came another of her thoughtful pauses; perhaps the sense of what Horton had said had only just sunk in. "But do you really think he didn't do it?"

The question had to come sometime, of course. She was looking at Maitland as she spoke. "I really do," he said, and glanced at Geoffrey, and smiled a little ruefully. Once for five minutes, I was sure, and now . . . "We need all the help we can get."

Cathie was following her own train of thought. "It isn't that I want 'an eye for an eye' . . . really, it isn't that. I pushed Mum into going to identify her, you know, when I saw the description in the papers, but that isn't why."

"Why, then?"

"Because I think . . . people . . . ought to know—"

"One person in particular? One of her friends, perhaps?"

"I'm not sadistic," she said, suddenly very much on her dignity. "I don't like watching people suffer."

"Now, what do you mean by that?" Maitland was feeling his way cautiously. Geoffrey had gone to the window and was craning his neck to see along the narrow alleyway into the court beyond.

"Unrequited love." Her voice was expressive, it mocked the phrase, even while it allowed an undercurrent of seriousness. "I thought—I didn't want her to be dead, of course—but I thought if she was, he ought to know."

"You're taking me around in circles. Who ought to know?"

"Tom Kinglake. He was in love with her, you see, and I told him all the things you suggested just now . . . that she'd gone off with some man, something like that. But it didn't make any difference. He just kept on."

"I see. Does Mr. Kinglake live in Streatham too?"

"Yes. He has a flat in one of those new blocks near the common."

"Tell me about him."

"I see him at the tennis club, but only occasionally; he often goes away during the school holidays. Or bowling. And sometimes he comes to the house, but it's usually just to talk about her." For the moment she seemed to have forgotten her qualms about answering questions, and if Maitland had any of his own about using her—considering what they were trying to prove—he did not display them. "He's a teacher—mathematics—and sometimes I don't think he can be a very good one."

"Why not?" (The stiffness of Geoffrey's back declared his disapproval as clearly as any words could have done. It wasn't as if Antony had no experience of controlling a witness, but here he was, letting the girl run on.)

"He's too nice," said Cathie confidingly.

"Anyway, he knew Molly very well."

"He wanted to marry her." Was there an *arrière-pensée* there, or could it be taken as a simple affirmative? "He used to take her out when he could afford it, and he often came to the house, and sometimes Molly would be in, and sometimes she wouldn't. He helped me get my 'O' levels, as a matter of fact, but she was having so much fun, I daresay it wasn't reasonable to expect her to give it all up."

"She did give it up, though. She went away."

"Yes, but . . . you mean, perhaps she went with somebody who would give her an even better time?"

"Something like that."

"Well, Tom wasn't the only one she went with, you know."

"You told me she had dozens of friends," said Maitland, and she had a quick smile for his mournful tone.

"There were two special ones," she said. "Bill Stoddard and Charlie Wolsey. I think she liked them both a lot."

"Did they want to marry her too?"

"I don't know. I should think so, but I don't *know*. Bill went away before Molly did . . . six months before, about. Of course, he might have asked her, and if she said no, that was why he went." She dwelt on this picture for a moment, obviously approving its latent drama. "And Charlie left Streatham too . . . I don't know when, exactly, because I didn't see him after Molly went away."

"Do you think he went with her?"

"She might have gone to join Bill, or she might have gone with Charlie. But I can't see why. I thought perhaps it was somebody new, somebody we didn't know about. A married man, perhaps."

"And you never heard from her again?"

"Just once. She sent me a postcard: *Tell Mum not to*

worry, we're getting along fine. Of course, she did worry, just the same."

"Didn't you?"

"Not to say worry. I think I was more hurt than anything. But I thought there must have been some very good reason for her going like that."

"What reason, for instance?"

"I wish I knew." Her eyes were fixed on a point behind his shoulder. They had a dreamy look. "Some great love."

Maitland allowed her to continue in her reverie for a moment before he said, "A postcard . . . I suppose there was no address?"

"Just the postmark, 'Brightsea,' clear as clear. And the card itself was called 'The Promenade at Noon.' "

"Brightsea again?"

"I . . . well, I thought so."

"Did you keep the card?"

"I brought it with me." She delved into her handbag and produced it, brightly colored, a trifle the worse for wear, and sat holding it as though it were a hostage. "Mr. Maitland, when the trial comes on . . . will all the mystery be cleared up?"

"That's a tall order. Between us, we shall try to do that."

"And you don't think this Dr. Langton is guilty? I thought he must be, if he was arrested, but I can't see what Molly had to do with him at all."

One way or another, she was going to get hurt. He didn't like the prospect, he didn't see how to avoid it. He said lamely, "Four years is a long time."

"You mean, she must have had lots of friends I didn't know. She may even have been married, her postcard might have meant that; but I can't see why she should keep us in the dark about it."

"We must work with what we've got." That was more for Geoffrey's benefit than for Cathie's. "Tell me about—Bill Stoddard, did you say?"

"He worked in a bank. He was always saying how badly paid they were. But his people had money, they lived in one of those big houses in Majorca Road. I suppose that was why he always seemed to be able to give her a good time."

"So he was transferred to another branch?"

"No, he left the bank. I don't know why. I suppose he found a better job."

"Did Molly hear from him after he left Streatham?"

"Well, he didn't write to her at home, I'm sure about that. Of course, she might have had a letter at the shop." She paused, but then anticipated his question. "She was a hairdresser. Myra's Beauty Salon. In the High Road."

"I see. The other man you mentioned—?"

"Charlie Wolsey. He worked for the local undertaker, and there was some talk when he went away, I remember, because he hadn't told anyone he was going, and he'd seemed settled enough."

"Talk among your friends, you mean?"

"That's right. I don't know if anyone bothered to ask his parents."

"And there was nothing like that about Stoddard?"

"Not that I remember. I expect his close friends knew where he was going."

"That would include Molly, wouldn't it? Did she tell you—?"

"Not a word. But then, I never asked her, you know."

"Did she seem depressed at all?"

"After Bill left? No . . . no, I don't think so. Afterwards I thought there had been a sort of excitement about her before she went away. But that might have been just imagination."

"Did your mother go to the police?"

"Well, she did, but I don't know what they could have done, after all. Molly was twenty-five, and she packed her bag and went. We never heard any more about it; I don't think they regarded her as a 'missing person' at all."

"I'm sure they didn't. Did you ask at her place of business?"

"At Myra's. Oh, yes, we asked, but she didn't know anything. Molly never even gave in her notice . . . ever so put out, Myra was."

"That seems to be that, then. Are you going to show me the postcard, Miss Armstrong?"

"Yes, I forgot." She held it out to him. Blue sea, blue sky, the corner of a kiosk selling ice cream, a stretch of yellow sand beyond the railing, a group of girls whose dresses made a splash of vivid color. The promenade at any one of a hundred places around the coast. The message written in a firm, round hand, and the postmark—what had Cathie said?—clear as clear. "Brightsea 18 11 61."

"Silly thing to keep, wasn't it?" she said gruffly.

"How long after Molly left home was this written?"

"A month, about."

"So it's a little over four years. She said she was a widow . . . did you know that?"

"Yes, they told Mum about it. She had to say we didn't know whether Molly had been married or not."

Geoffrey had turned from the window and was regarding them in a disapproving silence, but he did not attempt to interrupt. "Well, Miss Armstrong," said Maitland formally, "you've been very helpful—"

"What are you going to do now?"

"Try to find out where Molly went after she left home."

"Do you think you can? You'll tell me, won't you?"

"I'm afraid you'll have to be content with one answer to both your questions. I don't know."

"I suppose it doesn't matter, really, but I think I'd feel better somehow."

"If I can tell you, I will. And, Miss Armstrong—"

"Yes?" She was on her feet now, and he had the imaginative fancy of a bird poised for flight.

"If you think of anything else, anything that might tell us where she went—"

"I've thought about it so much, I don't suppose I can think of anything new. All the same, if this doctor didn't do it—"

She paused for so long that he prompted her at last. "Well?"

"I wouldn't want him to be—to be convicted. I'd feel guilty about that myself."

"There's nothing for you to worry about, you know."

"Isn't there?" She sounded doubtful. "If I hadn't made Mum go to the police station, none of this would have happened. And to tell you the truth, Mr. Maitland," she added seriously, "I don't believe Tom's a bit happier now he knows."

"That was hardly to be expected." His tone must have conveyed more sympathy than his words, for she grinned at him suddenly and said quite cheerfully, "Don't tell me to be patient. He'll get over it. I know!"

With that she was gone. No conventional farewell, an impression of unfinished business. Geoffrey only just managed to catch up with her as she was going down the stairs.

Friday, 2nd July

Maitland went to Oakhurst the first available day, which happened to be Friday, and Horton went with him. All the freshness had gone from the air now; it was a stuffy day, cloudy with occasional sun. And already the neat garden at Oak Dene had acquired a neglected look, while the shrubbery brooded as dark and sinister as before . . . a fancy which Horton condemned as nonsense, thereby nearly ruining the expedition at the start. Maitland—almost in agreement with his friend concerning the foolishness of the inquiries he was bent on making—was in no mood to tolerate criticism. He had been making plans for the long vacation, but it seemed altogether too far off.

They had to wait for ten minutes or so until Dr. Bannister dismissed his last patient. The doctor turned out to be a sandy-haired young man with a self-confident air about him; not quite so self-confident as the interview progressed.

"How long have you been associated with Dr. Langton?" Horton asked.

"Almost three years."

"In that case, you must have known Mrs. Ruth Langton."

"Yes, quite well." (Maitland was prowling, which Ian Bannister obviously found distracting.) "I didn't live at Oak Dene until after her death."

"Did you like her?"

"Very much. She was . . . it wasn't easy for her, you know. She was very patient."

"You are speaking now of the progress of her illness."

"Yes. I wasn't her doctor, but it was obvious enough."

"I thought," said Maitland, apparently intent on something that was happening in the garden, "you might be referring to her relations with her husband." There was a silence after this remark, and after a moment he turned with an eyebrow raised inquiringly.

"What the devil is interesting you so much out there?" asked Geoffrey with ill-disguised irritation. Antony smiled at him.

"Nature," he said. "The flowers are growing . . . at least, I suppose they are. What could be more exciting? Are you going to tell me, Dr. Bannister," he went on, with no change of tone, "or are you going to intimate, unoriginally, that there are certain things a gentleman does not say?"

"I expect you want the truth," said Ian unwillingly.

"If you say anything at all . . . yes, of course."

"You're supposed to be on Henry's side."

"I have, all the same, a certain odd preference for knowing the worst."

"Her condition varied. She was never very well, and sometimes she could hardly get about at all. You mustn't think he was ever impatient with her; I never saw him anything but kind. But I think—I know—he was under a terrible strain."

"Did you know he had fallen in love with the present Mrs. Langton?"

"I didn't *know.*"

"If you were giving evidence in court, the prosecution wouldn't leave it there."

"Well, then, I guessed. I've known Susan forever, you see. Besides, there was talk."

"I can imagine." He turned back to the window again. "I'm sorry, Geoffrey. Your witness."

Horton went back to the point they had left. "Was it Dr. Langton's suggestion that you should come here to live?"

"It was. He seemed . . . I thought he would like the company."

"And you have lived here ever since?"

"Until . . . until the time of Henry's arrest. I'm staying at the Angel at the moment."

"What arrangement did you have concerning free time?"

"We took alternate weekends, unless there was an epidemic . . . something like that. And I used to go home after surgery on Tuesday morning—to my parents' home in Golders Green, that is—and return in time to take the Wednesday-morning surgery."

Maitland halted his pacing, halfway between chair and window, as though a thought had suddenly struck him. "Was this Dr. Langton's consulting room?"

"Yes. It's more convenient for me to use it because—"

"The blind cord has been replaced."

"Yes."

"Had you noticed it was missing?"

"No, I hadn't."

"And yet you were frequently in here, I suppose."

"Yes, very often."

"Good. Now—bear with me a moment, Geoffrey—let us postulate that Dr. Langton murdered one of the patients, say, at his Tuesday-evening surgery, when you were safely out of the way, and concealed the body . . . behind that screen, perhaps, it seems to be the only place . . . would you think he could have done this without the housekeeper's knowledge?"

"He could have done, but if Mrs. Jackson looked in, she'd have been bound to notice if the screen was out of place, and ten to one she'd have done something about it. She was a—compulsive tidier-up."

"Better and better. Can you think of any other place of concealment?"

"No."

"Thank you. We'll take the supposition a little further. All this having happened on a Tuesday night, and Dr. Langton having had the luck to get away undiscovered, could he have moved this—this hypothetical body to the garden and buried it there, without Mrs. Jackson's knowledge?"

"I think he could. Only if the telephone rang by his bed, and went on ringing—"

"She would have heard it and gone to investigate."

"I'm sure she would." He hesitated. "There is one thing, though. If he'd gone out on a sick call—"

"Well?"

"The routine was to switch the phone extension through to her room. That way it wouldn't disturb her unless there was a call while he was gone. If that happened, she'd have to get up, of course, to leave a note in his room. But she wouldn't think there was anything strange about finding him gone."

"I see. Did you know Molly Browne, Dr. Bannister?"

"She was a private patient, and Henry treated her the few times she came in."

"He said you'd look it up for us."

"No need to, I've already done so. I was interested, of course. One time she came in with a sore throat; another, she wasn't sleeping. He prescribed on both occasions, but from his notes, I imagine he thought her a bit of a hypochondriac."

"Did it strike you as odd . . . that she wasn't on the National Health, I mean?"

"No, it didn't. Quite a lot of people prefer it that way."

"Had you met her socially?"

"Yes, a good many times, though I can't say I knew her well. She was immensely attractive, you know, and just a little bit too conscious of the fact. And I'll tell you one thing, I've thought since, it must have taken great determination to—to deliberately wipe out so much vitality. Not Henry's kind of thing at all."

"That's very interesting." Ian glanced at him suspiciously. "No, really, I mean it. It won't carry any weight with the jury, of course, but I find it . . . comforting." He sat down for the first time and pulled an old envelope out of his pocket, and began to write, clumsily, on his knee. "One other thing, Dr. Bannister . . . about the night Ruth Langton died."

"I was here, playing bridge. I left when Mrs. Harper did, at ten-fifteen."

"You remember that exactly?"

"I couldn't forget it. I went over it often enough with the police."

"So you also know when Dr. Langton went out."

"Just before ten. I offered to take the call, of course, but he wouldn't hear of it. Anyway, I didn't have my car."

Maitland was still scribbling industriously. "Is there anything else, Geoffrey? I expect Dr. Bannister wants to be getting on his rounds."

"I think you've covered everything," said Horton, with some amusement in his voice.

"Then we mustn't keep you. I should think you're having a pretty rough time just now."

"I'm busy, yes. But everyone is at great pains to be nice to me," said Ian bitterly. And added, in a much more natural tone, "They make me sick!"

"Envy, hatred, and all uncharitableness," said Maitland vaguely, and stuffed the envelope back into his pocket again.

"That's just about it. Susan has been splendid, but it's hell for her, you know."

"I can see it must be, but there's no way out of it, I'm afraid."

Bannister left then. "Not much doubt where his sympathies lie," said Geoffrey as they went to look for Susan Langton.

They found her upstairs, sorting through the contents of the linen cupboard in a determined way. There were changes in her, as there had been in her husband. Her pallor no longer looked healthy, and her calmness was obviously as brittle as fine-spun glass. She left her task with patent relief. "I'm so glad to see you both. Is there any news?"

"Only what you already know," said Geoffrey regretfully. "Molly Browne has been identified, and the prosecution will contend that the alibi was a fake."

"And so he killed her." She looked from one of them to the other. "It's so unbelievable, if you knew Henry. But you don't, of course."

"No," said Maitland, watching her. He wondered if she was quite as positive as she was trying to sound.

"Is it what *you* think?"

"No," he said again, and smiled at her. "He's told us an incredible story, Mrs. Langton . . . a story the jury will find incredible, unless we can prove it is true."

"I don't understand."

"Tell her, Geoffrey." He moved a little away from them, and leaned back against the railing at the head of the stair. Too pretty to make a good witness, too easily trapped, perhaps, into dangerous admissions. But it was her looks that were the main objection . . . a motive for Ruth Langton's murder paraded before the jury, without even the need for the prosecution to point it out. Not that they would be slow to do so. . . .

Horton was finishing his explanation; doing it, too, without open incredulity, which was decent of him, as things were. "So you see, Mrs. Langton, the second murder remains the pivot of the case. Did your husband ever say anything to you, or do you know anything of your own knowledge, that would help us there?"

"Nothing at all." She sounded shaken, bewildered. Was there anything to be surprised at in that?

"Did he ever speak to you about Molly Browne?"

"There was never anything to say. I knew what happened after Ruth died, of course . . . everyone in Oakhurst knew that. But Henry and I weren't—weren't talking confidentially at that time. Not for some time afterwards, I told you that."

"So you did. Who was most intimate with her, do you know?"

"Mrs. Harper, I should think. She lives in the house at the top of the High Street, near the common. Number thirty-seven." She paused, and then went on in a rush, "You won't tell her . . . what you've just told me, will you? I don't think she'd understand."

Horton started to protest, but Antony smiled at her again and said gently, "We shall just ask her some questions, and madden her by not giving out any information at all."

"You mustn't think . . . it's different, knowing Henry as I do." (I was right about that, she's beginning to have doubts herself.)

"Our case will be that Molly Browne was brought here and buried during the time you were away on your honeymoon. After that, you'd have known, wouldn't you, if Dr. Langton had gone out at night when there hadn't been a sick call?"

"I'd have known, of course. There was never anything like that."

"The medical evidence will be vague. There is some reason to think she was killed on a Tuesday, so Dr. Bannister's evidence is negative, at best. We shall have to see Mrs. Jackson—"

"I wish you didn't have to. She's spiteful. I don't think she ever liked Henry at all."

"Don't worry, Mrs. Langton. I expect her evidence will be negative, too, but if we can use it, we shall call her, of course."

"I see." But she shook her head, as though the idea made

her uneasy. "I could tell them there was never anything—anything odd in Henry's behavior. He couldn't have hidden it from me."

"No, I'm afraid—" She'd no idea, of course, of the sort of questions she'd be letting herself in for. "Best leave it to us. You can rely on Mr. Horton, you know; everything possible will be done."

"I know that. It's only . . . I wish I could help."

He thought she was doing a pretty good job, just by staying sane. "You're holding things together."

"But what's the use? What's the use, if he never comes back?"

"I asked you last time we were here if you were lonely. Don't you think—?"

"I couldn't bear it. There's nobody who believes in Henry now. Even Ian . . . I don't know if he's just being kind. Please, Mr. Maitland . . . I'm really much better alone."

"And we must leave you." He straightened himself and turned toward the head of the stairs. "One last question, though. When you came back from your honeymoon, was there any sign that somebody had broken into the house during your absence?"

"It was all quite tidy . . . too tidy, really. Henry leaves things about, you know, but Mrs. Jackson always clears up after him. So I didn't notice anything out of the way, and I'm sure she would have said quickly enough if she had."

"The blind cord was taken, and one of Dr. Langton's handkerchiefs. You might have noticed if the blind cord was missing from the surgery."

"I might have done, but I didn't. I can't think why there are venetian blinds on those windows, Mr. Maitland; the shrubbery makes the room so dark, I don't think there's any need for them."

"So it was quite natural that Dr. Langton didn't notice either."

"Quite natural. And, of course, a handkerchief . . . anyone could have found one easily, they're in the top drawer of the tallboy. And whoever would miss a thing like that?"

"What about the drawing room?"

"That's different. I like the sun myself, the carpets just have to take their chance, but I daresay Ruth was more careful."

"And the man who said he saw a shadow on the blind the night she died"—Susan closed her eyes for an instant as though she found the picture too ugly to contemplate—"was that possible?"

"Oh, yes. They were the other kind of blinds, you know, light-colored, and with a sort of lace edging . . . pretty grim. They've been taken away now, but the police came around and tested one night, Henry said."

"To go back to the question of Molly Browne's death and the handkerchief that was found clutched in her hand, there remains the problem of getting into the house."

"One of the downstairs windows. I'll come down with you and show you. I'm sure anybody could open one of them from outside with a penknife, or something like that."

"We'll let Mr. Horton try it," said Antony, standing aside to let her pass. And, in fact, it did prove to be quite easy, but there was nothing whatever to show that an entrance had been forced that way.

"There's a Yale lock on the front door," said Susan stubbornly. "They could have left the window locked and gone out that way."

"Of course they could. Don't worry." But he was frowning as they walked down the drive to the gate. "You know, Geoffrey, I've a nasty feeling that I should also have said, don't hope."

/ 2 /

They had an early lunch at a café which evidently considered hunger to be vulgar, and was consequently unwilling to go even halfway toward satisfying it. After that they walked up the High Street and sat on a bench at the edge of the common until it seemed a suitable hour to call on Mrs. Harper. "As long as she doesn't go in for an afternoon siesta," said Maitland gloomily. He had found it depressing to be required to make a choice between sardines on toast and a poached egg.

He needn't have worried. Mrs. Harper was a bustling woman, perhaps twenty pounds overweight and feeling the burden, but still full of energy. Antony had been in some doubt about their reception, but that was satisfactory, too. "I always liked Henry Langton," said Mrs. Harper firmly, looking from one of them to the other as if daring them to contradict. "So if there's anything I can do, anything at all—"

"There are a few questions."

"You'll be wondering at me saying that, and not being at Oak Dene to look after Susan. Well, I daresay if it weren't for Jane Desmond, I should be there, but you can't expect the girl to say 'No' to her own mother and then let me stay with her, can you now? And I can understand her not wanting Jane, because it stands to reason she couldn't put up with hearing her complaining morning, noon, and night. Nothing that Henry ever did was right, so now—you can imagine!"

"I can indeed," said Maitland sympathetically. He was inclined to like Mrs. Harper, for all she was so garrulous, and he plunged straight into his questions, without waiting, as he generally did, for Geoffrey to break the ice. "It seems you knew Molly Browne as well as anyone in Oakhurst, Mrs. Harper."

"Yes, I think I did. She was a nice girl, Mr. Maitland." She broke off and sighed. "I'm not sure now if I ought to say, she *seemed* a nice girl. But at the time she didn't know anybody here, and it was only kind to introduce her to as many people as I could."

"How did you first meet her?"

"It was at a church bazaar. I was looking after the white-elephant stall, and we got talking, and she told me she was living at Rose Cottage, and I asked her to come and see me."

"Do you remember when that was?"

"Oh, yes, it was early October. Nineteen-sixty-three, it must have been. She said she'd been in Oakhurst for a week, I remember that."

"*Mrs.* Browne, she called herself?"
"I understood she was a widow. Well, I'm sure she told me that, though she didn't talk much about the past."
"Did she say where she had been living before she came here?"
"No. No, I don't think so. She mentioned Scarborough once, to say how cold it was in the winter; but I don't think she said she'd ever lived there."
"Was she employed in any way?"
"No, she seemed in quite easy circumstances."
"What about her other friends?"
"I introduced her to as many people as I could, and then I met her at other houses sometimes, so I don't think she was lonely. She was such a bright, happy person, I'm sure she always helped to make a party go."
"Was there anyone with whom she was especially intimate?"
"Someone nearer her own age?" pondered Mrs. Harper. "There was Susan, but I think they were only friends in a casual way."
"Any men friends?"
"No, and my impression was that she discouraged them. I thought perhaps it wasn't long since she had lost her husband—though she was always cheerful, I will say that."
"Did she know Ruth Langton?"
"I'm sure she must have met her here sometimes."
"Did you ever get the impression that she was unduly interested in other people's affairs?"
"We all enjoy gossip, Mr. Maitland, don't we? I don't think you could say Molly was unduly interested, not really."
Better put the question plainly. "Do you think she would have heard the Langtons spoken of?"
"No one would say a word against Henry in *my* hearing," said Mrs. Harper belligerently. "But I'm afraid it was obvious, you know, that he wasn't happy. And then Ruth, getting about with such difficulty. I think it's all too likely that someone explained the position to Molly. I've heard comments, myself, before I put my foot down."

"Did you ever visit her at Rose Cottage?"

"Only once."

"By invitation?"

"Well, no. I was collecting for the Organ Fund."

"Did she make you welcome?"

"She gave me a pound note, and then we had some tea. But when I think about it, I don't know that she was all that pleased to see me. Perhaps I shouldn't say that—"

"I'm very grateful for your impressions, Mrs. Harper."

"Well, then, she seemed uneasy. Nothing that was said, or done . . . more an atmosphere, really."

"Perhaps she wasn't used to entertaining?"

"It seemed like that, but she was quite a self-possessed person, you know. Not at all ill-at-ease in company."

"Did you have the impression that she had other visitors? Someone to stay with her, perhaps. Or just casual visitors like yourself?"

"I can't say I thought about it, but now you mention it, I don't remember ever hearing of anyone who went to see her. But it was a furnished cottage, not terribly comfortable. I daresay she wasn't too keen on asking people there."

"How long did she stay in Oakhurst?"

"Nearly six months. She came to see me at the beginning of March, to say good-bye."

"Where was she going, did she say?"

"No. I asked for her address, of course, but she said her plans were uncertain, and she'd send me a note as soon as she was settled. Oh, and she said 'now that spring is coming.' I had the impression she might be going north."

"Back to Scarborough, perhaps."

"She didn't say."

"Did you hear from her again?"

"No, and I wondered about it, of course. But people do that, don't they? I daresay at the time she meant to write, and then she was busy."

"You didn't hear of her visiting Oakhurst in the early part of this year?"

"You're thinking she might have come to see somebody, when she was killed. It might be so, of course, but I didn't hear anything about it."

"I see. Now, one other thing, Mrs. Harper. The night Ruth Langton was murdered—"

"Poor Ruth. She seemed well that night . . . well for her, that is. And even at the worst, she'd come to terms with her illness. Not so much resigned to it, as making the best of what she had."

"What was her relationship with her husband?"

"She loved him. And I'll never believe that Henry would have done anything to hurt her."

"So everything was as usual that evening."

"Yes. We were playing bridge. Even the phone call, there was nothing surprising about that."

"Did Dr. Langton say where he was going?"

"No. Ian Bannister offered to go for him, and he just said, 'one of my crosses, Ian,' and that he'd be back as quickly as he could. But it was nearly ten o'clock then."

"How long did you stay?"

"Perhaps twenty minutes. It was a quarter past when we left. I didn't want to stay any longer, because Ruth used to get tired."

"Did you think she would go straight to bed?"

"I should have expected her to, but she might have decided to sit up for Henry. There's no telling either way."

"Did Dr. Bannister leave when you did?"

"Certainly. I had a taxi, and I offered to drop him off at his lodgings, but he said it wasn't far, he'd enjoy the walk."

"Mrs. Harper, had you at that time heard any gossip about Henry Langton and Susan?"

She sat silent for a moment, looking at him. It was odd, really, that this was the first time she had questioned the trend of his remarks. "I thought . . . I understood . . . you were trying to help Henry."

"We are."

"That won't do him any good. In any case, I told you *I* wouldn't have heard."

"It won't help him if the evidence is available, and the prosecution spring it on us at the trial."

"Well, then, I could see how things were between them. I don't suppose I was the only one."

"You think it would have formed a subject for comment."

"Yes, oh, yes. I'm sure of it."

They left soon after that, and went back to the bench near the common again, to talk things over. "I'd have liked to see the neighbor," said Antony in a thoughtful way. "You say the prosecution are calling her?"

"To identify the photograph, yes, they are. And a Mrs. Plackett, from the shop where Molly Browne bought her groceries."

"What did she have to say for herself, anyway? The neighbor, I mean."

"'I didn't know her well, but we'd meet at the shops sometimes, and once or twice she came in to have coffee with me,'" said Geoffrey precisely.

"Anything about visitors?"

"Nothing. She doesn't overlook Rose Cottage, you know."

"I suppose we could go and look at the place for ourselves."

"We could, but it won't do any good."

"What about the estate agent?"

"She paid monthly, in advance, and gave a banker's reference. Lease was minimum six months, started the first of October, ended the thirty-first of March; they've no idea of the precise date she took possession, or when she left. And the bank—I suppose that's your next question—had handled the account for nine months. She opened it by paying in two thousand pounds, and had made regular monthly withdrawals ever since."

"How much?"

"One hundred pounds."

"Has she still got a balance there?"

"No, she drew out what was left on the thirteenth of March last year."

"Suggestive, isn't it?"

"Only if you've made up your mind in advance," said

Geoffrey sourly. "By the way, you were wrong in what you said to Mrs. Langton. The housekeeper will be one of the Crown's witnesses."

"Damn. They aren't going to have any difficulty about this identification, are they?" he added hopefully.

"No such luck. Mrs. Armstrong is quite positive. There's an appendix scar; that wouldn't have done much good, but the birthmark on her foot—her shoes were a protection, you see—was quite clear and unusual. And afterwards, the dentist confirmed it, so that's tied up tight enough."

"I meant at this end."

"Not a chance. There's a photograph of her, a professional job—"

"Cathie said they kept it in a drawer."

"That doesn't mean it doesn't portray her features accurately. The witnesses are in no doubt at all."

"Damn the witnesses."

"If you like. I don't suppose it will make them any less certain."

"I don't suppose it will. What about Dr. Fielding? Are they calling him too?"

"If you'd take the trouble to read the papers I send you—" Geoffrey grumbled.

"I will, in due course. They look terribly dull."

"They *are* dull. They are also factual . . . so far as they go."

"A treat in store," Antony murmured. "Never mind, we'll console ourselves with a view of Rose Cottage. I don't suppose you'd like to take me to Streatham after that."

"I should not."

"It isn't far."

"You could catch a bus and be there in forty minutes," suggested Horton callously. Antony ignored him.

"Tomorrow, then."

"Oh, if you like."

"I'm grateful," said Maitland, suddenly formal. But then he grinned and added, "You got me into this, you know."

They went to see Rose Cottage after that; but, as Geoffrey had foretold, neither of them found it a source of inspiration.

/ 3 /

Sir Nicholas came upstairs that evening after dinner, apparently for the sole purpose of asking when the case came on. It was obvious, though, that he expected the answer to take some time. Antony watched his uncle produce, first a cigar, then his cigar cutter, and finally a box of Swan Vestas, and lay them on the table, conveniently to hand. "I suppose you'd like some brandy," he said, without much enthusiasm. He was tired that night, and his shoulder was hurting him.

"That, and an answer to my question."

Jenny already had the cupboard door open. Antony leaned against a corner of the mantel. "In about two weeks' time, as far as we can tell."

"Hm. Thank you, my dear," he added, as Jenny set down a glass at his elbow. His eyes moved back to his nephew's face again. "When last you spoke to me about it, you were inclined to take a sensible view."

"You mean, I thought my client was probably guilty."

"So I understood. However, Mallory tells me—"

"Mallory," said Maitland without rancor, "is an interfering old—" He broke off when he saw his uncle's smile.

"You are undoubtedly right," said Sir Nicholas gently. "I should be glad to know, however, precisely what line of defense you propose to follow."

"It's a little complicated."

"Beyond my understanding, perhaps."

"I only meant . . . oh, well, here goes. Langton maintains that he really was with Molly Browne when his wife was killed, but he let Molly take five thousand quid off him the next day to confirm the alibi."

This was enough to make Sir Nicholas sit up bolt upright in his chair. "I don't believe it," he said after a moment, and relaxed again, limply.

"That's what I said, but it's perfectly true."

"The lady appears to have been something of an opportunist."

"I don't think it was exactly that. She claimed to be suffering from fibrositis, but there was no sign of it the next day when he called on her. She also detained him deliberately beyond the normal length of a sick call."

"Siren tactics?" asked Jenny, placing a glass on the mantelpiece at Antony's shoulder, and going to sit down in her favorite place on the sofa.

"Not exactly, though she did play on his sympathy, I understand."

"What are you suggesting, then?"

"A deliberate plot, to murder Ruth Langton and leave her husband only one way out of the mess . . . by accepting the alibi. It couldn't have worked if he hadn't been perfectly well aware that he had the sort of motive that anyone can understand."

"What motive?"

"Two of them. Love *and* money."

"The payment of the blackmail can be easily demonstrated, I expect."

"He sold some shares through his bank, and drew out the proceeds in cash. Of course it can be demonstrated," said Antony, whose patience with this inquisition was wearing thin.

"You mustn't misunderstand me. I have nothing against your taking the case. I hope," said Sir Nicholas insincerely, "that I am not an unreasonable man. But to persist in this particular line of defense—"

"I happen to believe Langton's story, Uncle Nick."

Sir Nicholas' preparations had reached the point where the cigar was ready for lighting. He took his time about it and did not reply until he was sure that it was burning with an even glow. "If you tell it in court," he said at last, "the jury will believe one of two things: that it is a complete fabrication, or that he paid to have his wife killed. In either case, you'll be no better off . . . unless it's your ambition to give the prosecution a good laugh at your expense."

"They won't laugh."

"Why, has Lamb got the case?" Sir Gerald Lamb, who had been Solicitor General under the last administration, was a man well known for his melancholy outlook.

"He has. But I don't see that I have any choice, sir. Langton will be asked what he did with the money; you must see that. I mean, it's a sizable sum; he can't explain it away as current expenses."

"Then all I can say is, I'm sorry for you. What do you hope to achieve?"

"I don't exactly hope anything . . . yet." He twisted around to take up his glass in his left hand, and drank, and stood staring in front of him with rather a fixed expression. "I say, Uncle Nick, you've given me an idea."

"May heaven forgive me," said Sir Nicholas piously. "Whatever it is, I'd forget about it if I were you."

"No, it wants thinking over." He sipped his brandy again, and an amused look crept into his eyes. "It's a pity," he said, "that Inspector Conway was the investigating officer. I mean, I've never felt that he really appreciated me."

"Don't go near him!" said his uncle, now thoroughly alarmed. Antony smiled, and he added in a dissatisfied tone, "I can't think why you can never do things in a straightforward way."

Sunday, 4th July

After all, they didn't go to Streatham the next day. Geoffrey was waiting for a report from Cobbold's, the firm of inquiry agents to whom he entrusted most of his work in that line, and there wasn't much point in going ahead without it. Maitland complained, "They may be as pure as the driven snow, but you must admit they go about their work in a damned leisurely way." But Horton, who had his weekend's work in the garden pleasantly mapped out in his mind—a not too arduous program—and who didn't feel like arguing anyway, only shrugged. So Antony gave it up and went home too.

Ostensibly he banished the case from his mind for the rest of that day, but actually he was preoccupied and inclined to stare into space (which annoyed Sir Nicholas when they met at lunchtime). It wasn't until noon on Sunday that he made up his mind and telephoned Chief Inspector Sykes at his home.

"What can I do for you, Mr. Maitland?" He wasn't surprised; Sykes was never surprised at anything.

"Do you think you could persuade Inspector Conway to come and see me?"

There was a moment of silence. "Is it about the Langton case?" asked Sykes cautiously.

"It is."

"I thought you told me—"

"I did. But that was two weeks ago."

"I see."

"I wonder if you do. But about Inspector Conway—"

"I think it might be managed." There was no doubt now that caution had given way to amusement in Sykes's voice. "If he thinks you know something—"

"No, really, Chief Inspector . . . if I did, I wouldn't tell *him*."

"Hope springs eternal, Mr. Maitland."

"Well, play it how you like. I shall be grateful."

"When are you free?"

"I shall be in chambers all day tomorrow." He rang off, to find Jenny watching him frowningly. "Don't scowl at me, love. It doesn't suit you."

"But, Antony . . . Inspector Conway!"

"He may be able to help us." He smiled when he saw

that she still looked puzzled. "He may not want to, of course. Who lives may learn."

Horton telephoned a few minutes after three o'clock. "Someone's been working overtime. They just brought the report around by hand."

"That's good."

"Do you want to see it now?"

"If it's not too hopelessly inconvenient."

Geoffrey laughed at the politeness, which he knew well enough was only surface deep. "I'll come right away," he promised.

He arrived at about four o'clock. The house was quiet, with the lethargy of Sunday afternoon hanging heavily over it. Antony took him upstairs, and found himself speaking in a hushed tone as they went. Even in the big living room, with both windows wide, the curtains hung lifeless, and there did not seem to be a breath of air. Jenny had disappeared into the kitchen and was making a cheerful clatter there.

"I hope you're not expecting any dramatic revelations," said Geoffrey as he settled himself.

"From one of Cobbold's reports? I know better than that." He paused, giving Horton a chance to speak, and then said slowly, "All the same, you thought it worthwhile to bring it around on Sunday."

"It's teatime," Geoffrey pointed out. Antony shook his head at him. "Don't you believe me?"

"I might, if Joan wasn't such a good cook."

"Oh, well! There is something. I don't think it means anything, myself."

"If you are about to admonish me concerning the dangers of jumping to conclusions—"

"You might just remember it's a hazardous practice. Will you let me tell you this my own way?"

"How else?"

"All right, then. Thomas Kinglake is in the phone book—still at Streatham, as Miss Armstrong said—so I didn't have to worry them about that. The other two men she mentioned, William Stoddard and Charles Wolsey"—it was characteristic of Geoffrey that though he had the report in his hand, he did not need to refer to it—"are both living in the London area, though there seems to be no trace that either of them has been back to Streatham for several years. Stoddard is working for the Imperial Insurance Company, one of their salesmen, and Wolsey has a house at Finsbury Park, and seems to have done quite well for himself. In business on his own account as a joiner and cabinet-maker—funds seem to have come from an uncle who died. No mystery about either of them."

"What about their private lives?"

"Stoddard is unmarried, and Wolsey married six months ago."

"That's interesting."

"I'm glad you think so. I should have said it was perfectly natural, myself."

"If you must be reasonable! What else?"

"They're still working on it."

"Well, at least, why did they disappear?"

"The answer to that is quite simple, too. They didn't. Stoddard's parents knew all about his new job, and so did his friends and the secretary of the tennis club that Miss Armstrong talked about. I don't think his family have seen anything of him for the past two years at least, but that's another story, and not an unusual one. As for Wolsey, his parents are dead, and Cobbold's only found one chap he knew who'd heard about his plans. Apparently he was something of a socialist . . . enough to be embarrassed by the sudden acquisition of funds—inherited wealth, at that! —but not enough to refuse the legacy."

"I'm sorry to say this, Geoffrey, but you're becoming cynical." He pulled an envelope out of his pocket and looked at it frowningly. "Wolsey was the undertaker's assistant, wasn't he? I don't wonder he wanted to get away from the coffins."

"I suppose you want to see all these people," said Geoffrey gloomily.

"Of course I do. But you haven't come to the end, have you? Because I can't see—"

"Not quite. There's one thing I haven't told you."

"Bill Stoddard's address."

"So you noticed the omission, did you? He lives at Oakhurst . . . a flat in the High Street."

"But that means . . . well, what does it mean? You must admit, Geoffrey, it might mean anything."

"Or nothing."

"As you so rightly remark. But you don't have to dampen my enthusiasm."

"That's a matter of opinion."

"Do you suppose he met Molly Browne? Do you suppose he's the reason she went there?"

"I don't know," said Horton woodenly. "If you want the rest, they talked to Myra too—Myra's Beauty Salon, you remember?—but she couldn't tell them anything more than she originally told Mrs. Armstrong. Molly had left without telling anyone, and even after four years Myra is still sore about it. She didn't know anything about Molly's special friends, though she remembered one man who used to wait outside the shop sometimes for her to leave. Nothing had ever been said to indicate her plans, but it seems they can't have included taking employment, because she never asked for her cards."

"I suppose that means they haven't got any lead on where she was going."

"I'm afraid not. The trail's a bit cold after all this time."

"All the same, she was somewhere during those four years. It must be possible to find out where."

"Any suggestions?"

"Hotels and boardinghouses at Brightsea."

"That's a big job."

"We might get some help from the police. I've been talking to Sykes—"

"This isn't his case."

"No, but I thought he might use his influence to get Conway to come to see me."

"What on earth do you want to see Conway for? I don't know if it's proper for you to see him, anyway."

"I shan't ask him any questions. I want to enlist his help in getting Molly Browne's photograph in the papers with a request for information."

"What about the snap we have?"

"They could blow it up, I suppose. I don't think it would serve the purpose very well."

"I doubt if Conway will agree."

"He might. I'd have to give him our reasons for the request, of course."

"But . . . you must be mad," said Horton flatly. "It's bad enough your insisting on using this ridiculous story, we don't have to tell the prosecution about it in advance."

"That's up to Langton, don't you think? Will you ask him?"

"If he'll let you convey the gist of his statement to the police, in return for some quite problematical favor?"

"That's right . . . more or less. I'm gambling on his innocence, Geoffrey, I don't see why he shouldn't be asked to place a bet as well."

"But, Antony, I hoped—"

"I know you did. You hoped I'd be so discouraged by this time that I'd drop the whole thing."

"We can't present this story unsupported."

"Then we must find support. Think of Bill Stoddard! Doesn't he give you even a gleam of hope? And I think you'll find, you know, that Langton is just as determined as I am to tell the truth."

"If it is the truth," said Geoffrey unhappily.

"We're working on that assumption . . . remember?"

"But are you sure—?"

"Of course I'm not sure! But you'll find that Langton is set on using the story—true or false. These quiet chaps can be as stubborn as the devil."

Jenny brought in tea just then, which perhaps was just as well. By the time he left, Geoffrey had agreed, though reluctantly, to talk to his client first thing the following morning. So they went downstairs together in comparative amity. Antony pulled open the front door, and followed the other man out onto the top step. At the same moment, a dark young man who was paying off a taxi at the curb turned and came toward them.

He was very dark, tallish, and slightly built, with strongly marked features and mild brown eyes. At the moment, however, the mildness was not the first thing you noticed; he seemed to be in a state of considerable agitation. He came up the steps at a bound, looked from Horton, who was carrying his hat and gloves, to Maitland, more casually attired, and addressed himself to the latter with no hesitation at all.

"You must be the chap who has been worrying Cathie Armstrong," he said angrily. "Now she's been hurt, and I want to know what you mean to do about it."

"Hurt?" said Maitland sharply. He wasn't sure what he was expecting; certainly not the reply he got.

"Someone tried to strangle her last night," said the newcomer, no more temperately than before. "The police say it was a bag-snatcher, but *I* think it was because she talked to you. I didn't get it out of her till just now, though I knew something was bothering her—"

"Wait a bit! Where is Miss Armstrong now?"

"At home. She's bruised, of course, and in a state of shock, but not too badly hurt, apart from that."

"But what makes you think—?"

"I don't like coincidences. I've no idea what she said to you, of course, but I do know she's been worried ever since."

"All the same—" But he was never to finish his protest. Another taxi had pulled up behind Geoffrey's Humber, and Cathie Armstrong jumped out, turned to thrust some money into the cabby's hand, and ran across the pavement and up the steps to join them.

"Tom, don't be so *silly*," she said. She was certainly pale, though no more than was natural; and at the moment Tom looked far more shocked than she did.

Antony looked at the visitor with more interest now . . . Tom Kinglake, the chap who was "too nice" to be a schoolteacher? He was saying, with considerable energy, "You keep out of this, Cathie. You ought to be at home in bed, not gadding about town like this."

"What choice did you leave me? I don't know what idea you've got into your head."

"You're not safe to be out alone. I'm not going to let anyone impose on you, that's all."

The cabdriver, who had been watching them with an indulgent eye, heaved a sigh and drove away. Antony said, "Don't desert me yet, Geoffrey. You'd better all come inside." They followed him quietly now, though Tom still looked as if he were on the brink of another outburst. The study door was open; he wasn't sure if Sir Nicholas was out or not, but on the whole it seemed worth risking.

Here again, though the window was open, the air was still and dead. He steered Cathie to one of the armchairs, took his stand with his back to the empty grate, and waved a hand invitingly to the others. Tom crossed the room to stand beside Cathie's chair, and Geoffrey, after a moment's hesitation, took the chair at the other side of the hearth. "I don't really understand why either of you are here," he said.

"That's easy," Cathie told him. "I was talking to Tom, and he suddenly lost his temper and rushed out of the house, so I thought I'd better follow."

"In case he became violent," Antony explained. Looking at him, Geoffrey was irritated to see that his eyes were dancing and that he had given himself up to a simple enjoyment of the situation. "Follow that cab!" he added, obviously relishing the phrase. "Quite in the best tradition."

"It wasn't really like that," said Cathie; she sounded regretful, as though her imagination, too, was stirred. "I had to stop to get a scarf and leave a note for Mum. But I guessed where he was coming, of course."

"Never mind." He wondered briefly what lines the conversation had taken, to make this clear to her. "Tell me what happened. Are you much bruised?" The scarf knotted carefully around her neck looked odd on that sultry day.

"I already told you," said Tom, asserting himself. "And I still say it's your fault."
"Am I right in thinking you're Mr. Kinglake?"
"You are."
"Calm down, won't you? Have a cup of tea . . . a whiskey and soda . . . a cigarette—"
"Not just now, thank you."
"Then tell me, what am I supposed to have done?"
"You're exploiting her. That's obvious."
"In what way? No, really, I want to know."
"Getting her to give evidence for this fellow Langton."
"You're not being very logical, Mr. Kinglake. If Dr. Langton is guilty, who is supposed to have attacked Miss Armstrong?"
"I don't know. I just say it's a coincidence, that's all. Ever since she talked to you—"
"You said she was worried. I'm sorry about that. But won't you cease hostilities just for a moment and let her tell me in her own way?"
"Of course I'll tell you. Be quiet, Tom. Only I don't really know what happened, it was all so quick."
"First, why were you worried?"
"Because I thought . . . because you seemed to think Dr. Langton was innocent after all. And I thought it was my fault he'd been arrested; at least, it was Mum's evidence that connected him with Molly, and she'd never have given it if I hadn't made her."
"That doesn't make you responsible. We only want the truth."
"Not if it convicts him, and he didn't do it," said Cathie unreasonably.
Tom Kinglake said suddenly, curtly, "We had to know."
"Yes, that's what I thought. I'm sorry." Cathie was polite but bewildered. "I seem to be in a muddle."
"Tell me what happened to you then."
"Yesterday evening? I'd been to the pictures with Brenda, and she left me at the corner of Hopworth Road. It was very quiet, it's surprising how quiet the streets are when you're

walking; but then, just as I was passing the end of the Valley Footpath, someone came out and grabbed me from behind. It was horrible."

"Mr. Kinglake said you'd been strangled."

"That's right. He had his hands around my throat. But I don't know, of course, if it was just to keep me quiet, or if he meant to kill me. I lost consciousness for . . . well, I don't know how long. And when I came around, Mr. and Mrs. Clement were with me—they're neighbors—and my handbag had gone, which is a terrible nuisance because of *things*."

"Had the Clements seen anything?"

"They thought they heard someone running, but they didn't see a thing."

"So they took you home, I suppose."

"Yes, it was quite near. And Mum rang the doctor, and then the police. And they said it was a typical job, and the man hadn't meant to hurt me—though that seems a funny way of going about *not* hurting someone, if you ask me. And there wasn't much in my purse to make it worth his while, about two-pounds-ten, I suppose; and all the other things I had in it wouldn't be worth anything to anyone but me."

"And what did the doctor say?"

"That I was to take a tablet to make me sleep," said Cathie, grimacing, "and take it easy until the bruises were better, and not to worry. I'm not worried, but—"

"So long as you're here, I'd better take you home," said Tom abruptly.

"Just a minute. If you're feeling well enough, Miss Armstrong—"

"I feel perfectly well."

"—there are one or two questions I should like to ask you."

"Yes, of course."

"You said, 'he had his hands around my throat.' Are you quite sure it was a man?"

"Yes. Yes, I think I'm quite sure of that."

"Have you any idea how tall he was?"

"Middling tall. His hands were hard, not soft like a woman's would be. And very strong."

"Did you notice anything else that might help to identify him?"

"You mean, if he used some special kind of after-shave lotion, or something like that?"

"Well . . . did he?"

"N-no." She sounded doubtful. "Now you mention it, I seem to think there was a faint whiff of tobacco. But it wasn't Turkish, or Egyptian, or anything I could identify at all." She shook her head. "I do think that's a pity," she said.

"You felt his hands, but obviously you couldn't see anything. You smelled tobacco, but not a distinctive brand. Did you hear anything at all?"

She took her time to think about that. "A harsh sort of breathing," she said.

She was so obviously entering into the spirit of the thing that he couldn't help asking her, "Are you sure you aren't pulling my leg?"

"No, I'm not. I hadn't thought of any of this before, but now I remember. A harsh sort of breathing, as if what he was doing excited him," she said, and shuddered. "Ugh! I wish I hadn't remembered, after all."

"Well, now you can forget it again."

"I don't see how I can . . . ever." But that was a bit of deliberate self-dramatization, or so he thought.

"Let's start by talking of something else. Does Scarborough mean anything to you?"

"Not to me personally. Molly went there one year for her holiday."

"In summer?"

"Yes, of course." She hesitated before she went on. "I don't want to seem inquisitive, but why have you asked me all these questions? Do you think, after all, Tom may be right?"

"I think he's right, though illogical. Which means you must be very, very careful."

"I don't see that at all. You mean it's a sort of revenge?"

"That's not very likely, perhaps. It could be fear . . . something you know."

"But I don't . . . I've told you everything."

"Something you've forgotten," he suggested. "Don't worry about it now, but remember to take care."

"I'll take her home," said Tom. "As for this idea of yours that she's going to give evidence—"

"I've no choice about it," Cathie told him. "Isn't that right, Mr. Maitland?"

"Quite right." He smiled at her. "You'll have to attend at court, at least, in case we want to call you. But I should be sorry to make you do anything against your will."

"It isn't exactly—"

But before she could explain any further, the door opened and Gibbs, Sir Nicholas' butler—a saintly-looking old man with a disagreeable disposition—announced coldly, "Dr. Bannister," and went away, leaving the newcomer stranded a few feet inside the door, and the former occupants of the room temporarily paralyzed by the force of his displeasure.

Maitland was the first to recover himself. "Come in, Dr. Bannister."

"I didn't mean to interrupt anything. Shall I—"

"First, let me introduce you. Dr. Bannister, Miss Catherine Armstrong. She's wearing that scarf because someone tried to strangle her."

"I beg your pardon!"

"Someone tried to strangle her. This is Mr. Kinglake, who thinks it was my fault, though I don't quite know how he works that out. And Mr. Horton you already know."

If he had meant to disconcert Ian Bannister, he had gone the right way about it. He was staring at Cathie with his mouth slightly open, and gave only the vaguest nod in Tom Kinglake's direction to acknowledge the introduction. "Would you take Miss Armstrong and Dr. Bannister upstairs, Geoffrey," Antony went on, "and introduce them to Jenny? I want a word with Mr. Kinglake, but it won't take long. It will save us a trip to Streatham."

"I'm going to take Cathie home."

"Yes, of course, after we've had our talk."

"She isn't fit—"

"With a doctor in attendance? Miss Armstrong, if you'd rather go straight home—"

"No. No, of course not. I'm perfectly all right."

When they had gone, Tom Kinglake took the chair Cathie had vacated, but he was still looking mutinous. "I can't see what you want with me."

"I want you to tell me about Molly Browne."

"I suppose you mean Molly Armstrong. Anyway, you've talked to Cathie."

"I can't help feeling your viewpoint will differ a little from hers."

"Suppose it does?"

"Were you in love with Molly?"

"Did Cathie tell you that? It's true enough. That was four years ago."

"You asked her to marry you?"

"What if I did?"

"We'd get on a lot quicker, you know, if you stopped answering every question with another one. However, if you really want to know . . . if you did ask her to marry you, I should conclude that you knew quite a lot about the lady and could therefore give me the information I need."

"I'm not at all sure I want to do that."

"Don't you want to know who killed her?"

"This fellow Langton—"

"Let us assume for the moment that he is innocent."

"That's the story you've been feeding Cathie."

"I must say," remarked Maitland patiently, "she has a much more trusting disposition than you."

"That's what makes me so mad. She is only a child, and you're taking advantage of her."

"You're out of date, Mr. Kinglake. Or are you still seeing her in her sister's shadow?"

"I don't know what you mean."

"That Cathie has shown herself rather less childish than you have," said Maitland bluntly. For some reason, the remark seemed to please Tom Kinglake, rather than disconcert him.

"What do you want to know?"

"Our point of digression was whether or not you had asked Molly to marry you."

"Well, I did. She didn't say 'No' exactly. I thought perhaps when she'd had her fling . . . but then she disappeared."

"Without any word to you?"

"Yes."

"Or, so far as you know, to her family or any of her friends?"

"I don't think anybody knew where she went."

"What did you think?"

"I thought there was another man. Someone none of us knew. What else was there to think?"

"Did you hear from her again?"

"Not a word."

"That surprised you?"

"It—it tormented me, if you must have it."

"Go back a little, then. How did she spend her holidays?"

"She'd go to one of the resorts. Scarborough, Blackpool, anywhere she could have a good time."

"The last year—?"

"Torquay, as far as I remember. But that was in August; it was January when she went away."

"Time for a summer romance to have cooled, you think?"

"That's what I meant. But I don't know . . . how can I know?"

"What about her other friends, at home?"

"Bill Stoddard used to take her out a lot. He wasn't hard up, and he could give her a good time."

"Did you know he is living in Oakhurst?"

"Is he?" He stopped, thinking that out. "I suppose you're trying to make something of that."

"It's a fact that has to be taken into consideration, like any other. What other friends had Molly, when you knew her?"

"There was Charlie Wolsey she used to go out with too;

and a chap called Ashley had his eye on her, but I don't think she cared for him at all. The other two . . . yes, she liked them well enough."

"Did you think either of them might have been responsible for her going away?"

"I thought about it, of course, though I must say I don't see why. There was nothing to stop her marrying whoever she liked. Anyway, I thought she had been married, to someone called Browne."

"We don't know that. As far as I know, the police have found no record."

"She might have been living with him, just the same."

"You think she wouldn't have minded forgoing the marriage ceremony?"

"That's a rotten thing to say, isn't it? If she was in love—"

"With someone who was a stranger to you all?"

"Well, that's what I thought, but something has just occurred to me."

"Yes?"

"She always used to say she'd hate the fuss of a wedding. She said the guests had all the fun of it, not the bride, and she'd rather just slip away. So that may be what she did."

"With whom?"

"I don't much like saying this . . . it's only surmise, after all. But Bill went away a few months before she did."

"You think, then, she might have slipped away to join him."

"Why not?"

"Have you mentioned this to any other person?"

"Of course not; I've only just thought of it. But Bill, or another . . . there was nothing I could do about it, anyway."

"Not even when Cathie had a postcard—"

"She never told me that!"

"Perhaps she didn't think it would be much help. The postmark was Brightsea, but there was no address given."

"At least, I'd have tried to find her." He paused staring down at his hands. "It's too late now. Perhaps it was always too late."

There didn't seem to be much to say to that. Maitland went upstairs to fetch Cathie, and saw them both on their way. Horton stayed—his curiosity, for once, proving too much for him—and when Antony finally got upstairs again, he was having a second tea, with Jenny and Ian Bannister.

And, after all, when Jenny had got up and left them, there wasn't much that Ian could say to help. "Mrs. Harper said you were looking for clues as to where Molly Browne came from."

"Didn't I ask you about that? I meant to."

"Well, I can't be very much help, but it occurred to me that I'd heard her talking about the Lake District, in particular the area around Keswick. I did think she must have lived there once, or stayed there for some time."

"Did she mention anybody she knew there . . . any street . . . any part of the town?"

"I'm afraid not."

"Do you remember who she was talking to?"

"To Ruth Langton, I think."

"You think?"

"No, I'm sure. They were sitting together, and when I joined them, Molly fell silent, and though I tried a few gambits myself about the Lakes, I couldn't get her going again."

"I see."

"It's nothing, really, only I thought . . . I'm concerned about Henry, you know. And Susan is so very unhappy."

"It may tie in, Dr. Bannister, when we know more. I appreciate your anxiety, of course. And while you're here, there is one other thing. Do you know a man called William Stoddard?"

"Yes, I do. He sold me some insurance."

"How long has he lived in Oakhurst?"

"Well, I'm not sure. He was already there when I arrived."

"Do you think he met Molly Browne?"

"I think . . . I'm sure he must have done. He knows Mrs. Harper, and you've no idea how popular a bachelor can be. And they both belonged to the badminton club; I expect he saw her there."

"Thank you. That's very helpful."

Ian was obviously curious, but he restrained it well enough. "I must be going," he said. But he did not get up straightaway. "That girl—Miss Armstrong—I gathered her visit had something to do with the case."

"She's Molly Browne's sister."

"Is she really? They aren't much alike. I don't really understand what's been happening, but is she in danger?"

"I can see no reason why she should be."

"But you said—"

"Someone attacked her. It may or may not have anything to do with Molly Browne's death."

"A bit of a coincidence, surely?"

"Coincidences happen. I'm inclined to think, like you, that this isn't one, but I've really nothing to go on at all."

"Oh . . . well . . . I'd better be going," he said again, and this time he got to his feet. Geoffrey left with him, and Jenny came back into the living room, full of questions.

"She isn't in the least like a boy, and I think she's very pretty. But do you really believe that someone tried to kill her?"

"It would be safer to assume so. The trouble is, I don't think she's very impressed herself with a sense of danger."

"The other one was nice . . . Dr. Bannister. He hadn't met her before, had he? He seemed to like her."

"She already has one young man, which is quite enough to be going on with." He paused, and then qualified the statement. "At least, she's probably in love with him, and he seems to feel protective towards her. That should be half the battle, don't you think?"

"Is he nice?"

"I daresay. I haven't really had the opportunity to judge." He dropped heavily into a chair, and stretched out his legs luxuriously. "It's too early for a drink, but I'd like one just the same. At one time the situation looked promising, but people," he added thoughtfully, "can be very trying at times."

Monday, 5th July

Detective Inspector Conway telephoned Maitland next morning, and arrived in chambers, pursuant on the promise he then made, precisely on the stroke of two o'clock. He was a thin-faced man with a pugnacious jaw and a tight-lipped look of displeasure; which was fair enough, Antony thought; the encounter didn't exactly fill him with delight either. Accompanying the Inspector was Detective Sergeant Mayhew, another old friend, but of whom he had kinder memories. Mayhew was younger and heavier than Conway, and inclined to be shock-haired, where the other was neat. He had a stolid look, almost sullen at times, and a nice sense of humor which was not often displayed.

Maitland had lunched at his desk and gone on working, and pushed papers and plate hastily aside when his visitors were shown in. "I'm grateful to you for coming," he said, when the proper greetings had been exchanged—a trifle frigidly on Conway's part, but that was only to be expected.

"I understand, Mr. Maitland, that you have some communication to make to me concerning the Langton affair."

"Not exactly a communication, Inspector. More in the nature of a request. Quite a reasonable one," he added hastily, before the detective's disapproval should spill over into open antagonism. "Wouldn't you like to know where Mary Armstrong had been in the four years prior to her turning up as Molly Browne?"

"Our inquiries are proceeding along the usual lines. Any information will, I presume, be passed on to Mr. Horton in the usual way."

"Yes, no doubt. I'm not suggesting there's been any hold-up. The thing is, Mrs. Armstrong gave you a photograph of her daughter."

"She did."

"Which has already been identified by several people in Oakhurst."

"Certainly."

"That means it's a good likeness. But it hasn't been released to the press."

"As we already have sufficient identification . . . you said a request, Mr. Maitland. What exactly is it you want?"

"I thought perhaps you'd agree to release it, along with an appeal for information."

"And have everyone who's ever known her phoning in!"

Sergeant Mayhew stirred, and coughed. "Or writing silly letters, which is worse," he said sepulchrally.

"Give the dates you're interested in. Let's see . . . since January, 1961. She must have been somewhere."

"We know she was at Oakhurst. Anything else is irrelevant to our case."

"But it isn't irrelevant to the defense."

"There is nothing to prevent you from advertising in the normal way."

"That's twice you've used that word. The trouble is, nothing about this case is normal, by any stretch of the imagination."

"That doesn't surprise me," said Conway, with some asperity. "But only, if you will forgive my saying so, since you took a hand."

"For heaven's sake, Inspector, can't we meet for once without quarreling?"

"It takes two," said Sergeant Mayhew, and paused lovingly over the unoriginal phrase.

"Doesn't the possibility of Dr. Langton's innocence concern you at all?"

"If you said 'the possibility of his getting off with a clever defense,'" said Conway waspishly, "I should be inclined to agree with you."

Mayhew only shook his head, as though the whole affair saddened him. Maitland hung on hard to his temper. "When I've explained to you—"

"It is not merely a whim, then? You have some specific purpose?" Conway's expression had become even more forbidding.

"What do you think? You've studied Langton's bank account . . . of course?"

"Of course. That is quite reasonable in the circumstances." (It took so little, thought Antony sadly, to put Conway on the defensive.)

"The Crown will be asking him, then, to explain a withdrawal of five thousand pounds, made shortly after Mrs. Ruth Langton's death."

"That, among other things."

"Let's stick to that for the moment. The reason I'm so keen on tracing Molly Browne's past is that I think there was a deliberate plot to implicate him, of which she was part."

Mayhew gave another of his warning coughs, but, wisely perhaps, he did not speak. "Don't you think you'd better justify that?" said Conway, and listened with his most sardonic expression while Maitland tried to do so. "If you have actually persuaded yourself of the truth of this," he said when the tale was ended—but his tone left no doubt at all what he himself believed—"I can only say, I'm sorry for you. A wilder piece of fiction—"

"There's s-something else." His temper was gone now. For the moment he did not even regret its passing. "Have you h-heard that there was an attempt on C-Cathie Armstrong's life?"

"I've heard of the bag-snatching episode, of course. You're not suggesting that it is in any way connected—?"

"I d-don't like c-coincidences, Inspector."

"And I, Mr. Maitland, don't care for the implication that I am weak in the head," said Conway curtly, and came to his feet as he spoke. "I should need to be—don't you agree?—to take any notice of this rigmarole."

"Then you won't help me?"

"I have already told you that any information we receive will be passed on to the defense in the usual way."

Mayhew ambled after him to the door, and turned there to bestow on Maitland one of his rare smiles, and offer what solace was in his power. "If you found out where the girl had been, you might not like it," he said. "Good day to you, Mr. Maitland." It was only then that Antony realized Conway had gone without even the formality of a farewell. He began to think over the interview, and wonder how he could have made his story more convincing. It was nearly half an hour before he pushed the problem resolutely aside, and went back to work.

/ 2 /

Later in the afternoon he made two telephone calls: one to Susan Langton, who knew Bill Stoddard through the badminton club, and thought Molly Browne must have met him there; the other to Mrs. Harper, who was quite sure Bill and Molly had been invited together to her house on several occasions, but whether they'd talked to each other at all, she didn't know.

After that it was harder than ever to concentrate, until Geoffrey telephoned with the news that he had made an appointment with Stoddard for six o'clock at Oakhurst. "I'll come with you and take the bus back," said Antony, who was too used to being unable to drive himself to let the fact worry him, except when—as happened too often when he was tired—he found his shoulder painful.

Oddly enough, he'd forgotten that Geoffrey would be curious. He recounted his interview with Conway with no great enthusiasm, and was perversely annoyed when Horton refrained from commenting "I told you so." "So we're no better off," he said gloomily. "And the prosecution are presumably, by now, a little wiser than they were before."

"I don't suppose that matters at all." Geoffrey attempted a bracing tone, with singularly little success.

"If you mean, because the case is hopeless anyway, I don't see that that's much comfort," said Maitland, unconsoled.

"I did mean that. There's been a new development, by the way."

"Tell me the worst."

"The housekeeper saw a lady's handbag in a drawer in Langton's surgery, on the eleventh of March. It didn't belong to either Ruth or Susan Langton, and the woman from the shop, Mrs. Plackett, has identified it from its description as being like one Molly Browne used to carry."

"How on earth did the housekeeper remember the date?"

"How should I know? It isn't relevant, anyway. They came back from their honeymoon on the seventh . . . perhaps that helped to fix it in her mind."

"What does Langton say?"

" 'The woman must have been dreaming.' "

"I don't like it, Geoffrey."

"Neither do I. Unless Mrs. Plackett had the same dream, which isn't likely—"

"You'll have to make him tell you. Even Lamb might laugh at that explanation."

Bill Stoddard's flat turned out to be over the café where they had lunched the previous week. There was a separate entrance, and when they stopped outside his door on the first landing, the stairs went on to another flat above. It was still a few minutes to six, and Antony was wondering whether they'd be condemned to drinking tea downstairs while they waited; but the door was opened with very little delay.

Stoddard was a big man, an athlete still in fairly good shape. In his mid-thirties, with fairish hair, rather shaggy. Not an insurance type, thought Antony; but then, what did he know about that, after all? Stoddard seemed friendly enough, and if a faint undercurrent of caution ran beneath his welcome, that was only to be expected.

There were two windows in the room, one at each end. Maitland drifted toward one of them, and stood looking out while the other men seated themselves. Horton was explaining their presence, the questions they wanted to ask. "As you knew Molly Browne before she came to Oakhurst, it seemed to us that you were the best person to consult."

"Yes," said Stoddard. "Yes, of course." He looked unhappily from one of them to the other. "I used to know Molly very well, but that's a long time ago."

"You mean when you still lived at Streatham?"

"That's right."

"You left to take up different employment . . . your present position, in fact?"

"Yes."

"Did you keep in touch with her?"

"With Molly? No."

Not exactly a forthcoming type. Antony let his attention wander. The King's Head opposite; the Angel, where Ian Bannister was staying, a little farther up the street. "Why not?" Maitland asked, and turned to see Stoddard's expression change from casual to concerned.

"Because I thought . . . because she didn't especially want me to, I suppose." He pulled a packet of cigarettes out of his pocket, offered them, and then took one himself and began to draw on it heavily as soon as he got it lit.

"I should be very grateful, Mr. Stoddard, if you would amplify that a little. We are anxious to learn all we can—" But Bill needed no prompting now; for some reason he seemed willing to explain.

"I asked Molly to marry me before I left Streatham. She didn't seem to like the idea."

"There was someone else, perhaps?" He went back to his exposition. "We are anxious to learn what happened to Molly Browne during the four years after she left home. If you can help us—"

Stoddard seemed to find this comforting, or perhaps he was just glad to be getting away from personal questions. He leaned back in his chair, relaxed for the first time since they came in. "I didn't think there was anyone else. Not that she cared about."

"You knew her friends, of course."

"Of course."

"Have you any idea which of them she would have been likely to go away with?"

"But wasn't that with Browne . . . whoever he was? She told me—"

"Wait a bit! She told you she was getting married?"

"No, I didn't mean that. When I met her again . . . when she was living at Rose Cottage . . . she said she was a widow."

"I see."

"She said more than that, if you want to know. She told me she'd quarreled with her mother about marrying . . . Jack, I think his name was. She said she didn't want to get in touch with her family until her first sense of loss had worn off, because she'd know all the time her mother would be thinking 'good riddance' . . . something like that."

"She asked you, in effect, not to mention your previous acquaintance?"

"That was what it amounted to. Yes."

"Did you make any attempt to . . . take up your friendship where it left off?"

"Well, naturally I did. Not that I was thinking of marriage. She didn't encourage me."

"Did you ever visit her at Rose Cottage?"

"Once or twice."

"At her invitation?"

"No. Just dropped in casually, I suppose you'd say. I'll tell you something, though. It didn't feel like a widow's house."

"You mean, there was some evidence of masculine occupation?"

"No. No, I didn't mean that exactly. There was nothing to suggest . . . I don't really think I can explain."

"Was she pleased when you went to see her?"

"She *said* she was."

"Don't you think she meant it?"

"Not really. I thought perhaps . . . but she didn't seem to want for anything, you know."

"Not even for companionship."

"Not even for that." He paused to think it out. "I think that must be what I meant."

"How often did you see her while she lived at Oakhurst?"

"Quite often. Once or twice a week, I should say."

"Did you notice—did she seem especially interested in the Langtons' affairs, for instance?"

"I don't know. When we met, we generally talked about ourselves."

"What did she tell you?"

"Not much more than I've already said. Jack Browne was an accountant, and I gathered he'd been dead about six months."

"Where had they lived while he was alive? Surely she told you that."

"Oh, yes. They lived at Brightsea. She even mentioned the name of the house . . . Bayview, or something like that."

"Had they lived there all the time they were married?"

"She never mentioned anywhere else."

"Tell us about her friends at Streatham, then."

"I don't see why they should interest you."

"Because—well, because I rather doubt if Jack Browne ever existed."

"I don't see why she should have been telling me a lie."

"Let's just say she may have been. If you had to guess which one of them she favored—"

"That isn't easy. I mean, until she refused me, I quite thought I was the one."

"Think about it, anyway. There was a chap called Ashley—"

"Definitely not him."

"Charles Wolsey, then."

"No, I don't think so."

"Tom Kinglake."

"On a schoolmaster's pay? I don't think so," said Stoddard again. "Besides, he'd become a sort of friend of the family. She wouldn't have seen him romantically, you know."

"What friends did she make at Oakhurst?"

"You saw her everywhere, but I don't know that she made any particular friends."

Maitland moved away again, to the back window this time—from which he was amused to note that the Golden Pheasant and the Smith's Arms completed the flat's encirclement—and let Horton take up the questioning where he had left it. But it seemed that Stoddard had no more to tell them, either of facts or of opinions. They thanked him and came away.

"Disappointing," said Geoffrey, when they got back to the car. "And when you were expecting so much, too."

"Disappointingly prosaic," Antony agreed. He did not sound notably cast down. "He seems to have decided that Molly Browne was a gold-digger, doesn't he? I wonder if that's true."

"I'd be more interested to know whether this fellow Browne exists or not."

"Would you really? I don't think there's any doubt about that."

"You said just now—"

"Perhaps I did."

"So we're to take Molly's word for it. For that matter, how do we know that Stoddard was telling the truth?"

"We don't. That's what makes it so interesting." Geoffrey exclaimed impatiently. "I don't mean that Jack Browne is necessarily dead, or even that he was ever alive, under that name. But—even apart from the evidence of the postcard—I decline to believe that Molly was living alone all those years, at Brightsea or anywhere else. Browne may be someone we know, or someone we've never heard of, but the man definitely exists."

"Stoddard himself—"

"On the whole, I should say he was the most likely bet. But there's someone else who lives in Oakhurst, you know . . . another possibility."

"Who?"

"Dr. Ian Bannister. Hadn't you thought of that? If anyone was in a position to know about the Langtons' affairs—"

"Yes, I see."

"He had also an excellent opportunity of killing Mrs. Langton. Having seen both the doctor and Mrs. Harper off the premises, he had only to go back and say he'd forgotten something . . . some message for Langton, perhaps—"

"I see that, too. But that would seem to imply that Molly lived those four years at Brightsea alone."

"It's no different if Stoddard was her partner. And not

too difficult to pick up a train at Clapham Junction. It's barely an hour's run."

"I don't know why we're arguing like this," said Geoffrey reasonably. "It's still by far the most likely that Langton committed both murders himself."

"So it is," said Antony annoyingly. "I wondered when that would occur to you. I'll see you tomorrow," he added, and crossed the road to the bus stop before Geoffrey could think of a suitable retort.

/ 3 /

It was at about ten o'clock that evening that Joan Horton telephoned, in a state of great agitation. Geoffrey had been held up outside his garage at East Sheen—in broad daylight, too. Arm around his throat . . . momentary unconsciousness . . . wallet gone . . .briefcase gone. No, he was quite all right, really, only rather annoyed. . . .

Tuesday, 6th July

He was still annoyed the next morning ("anyone would think it was my fault," said Maitland plaintively), but he was worried as well. "I'm beginning to think you're right about Langton," he said, "but I don't see what the hell we can do about it."

"We do seem to be working ourselves into a dead end," Antony agreed. "The thing is, what does he want? First Cathie's handbag, now your briefcase."

"*And* my wallet."

"Camouflage. I don't suppose it was important at all."

"It was to me."

"Yes, I suppose. I'm really sorry, Geoffrey," he added

placatingly, "but you must see that the important thing is—"

"What does he want? You already said so."

"Well, what do you think?"

"The snapshot of Molly Browne," said Horton tentatively. "I can't think of anything else that might first have been supposed to be in Cathie's possession."

"It's gone, I suppose."

"Yes, of course. Along with a lot of other things."

"The postcard, for instance. The postcard from Brightsea."

"I'm afraid so. Do you think it was that—?"

"I don't know. Did you smell tobacco?"

"I wouldn't have noticed, would I? I smoke myself."

"A lot of people do. Including Ian Bannister, for instance; he smokes a pipe. I noticed the doings in his surgery."

"I don't think much of that for a clue," said Geoffrey frankly.

"It might be an indication . . . never mind. What do the police say?"

"Nothing reported in their area recently, but a very usual pattern for a crime of this sort."

"In daylight?"

"The garage is quite secluded, you know. Joan couldn't have seen anything from the house, nor could the neighbors. I asked the police to tell Inspector Conway, and he phoned while I was having breakfast this morning."

"What did he say?"

"That I ought to be more careful of the company I keep."

"Apart from the rudeness, if he meant that, he takes it seriously . . . don't you think?" He hesitated. "I think it's about time we had a talk with Sykes."

"What good will that do?"

"I don't know. At least, it can't do any harm."

They went to see Charles Wolsey that afternoon at his place of business; attractive because of the pleasant smell of timber, and the equally unmistakable odor of success. Wolsey himself seemed less at ease than Stoddard had been, his answers more cautious. He would hardly admit to knowing the Armstrongs, let alone to having been in love with Molly. Certainly she hadn't confided in him; if she'd gone away with anyone, it would have been Bill Stoddard. As for himself, he had never set eyes on her, or heard from her either, since the day she left Streatham. Yes, he had left himself soon after, when probate of his uncle's will had gone through.

"And the trouble is," said Maitland disconsolately, as they left after a difficult quarter of an hour, "everything he says is probably true."

He did not find the idea encouraging, and said as much to his uncle when they sat over coffee that evening after dinner. Horton was there too, his sensibilities in a fair way to being soothed by the combination of a good meal and Jenny's sympathy. They were waiting for Sykes. . . .

"I don't know how you can expect anything else," said Sir Nicholas idly.

"Oh, I think we've a right to expect a few lies. It would make things so much easier. I must say, I rather fancied the undertaker's assistant as the murderer, but I wasn't exactly hopeful," Antony explained. "I just hoped."

"That was still more foolish. Is your mind quite made up . . . do you intend to use this—this extraordinary defense?"

"My instructions are—" said Antony provocatively. Geoffrey rose at once to the bait.

"No, that's not fair."

"You said you'd begun to believe Langton's story."

"That's one thing. Parading it in court is another."

"Have you asked Langton?"

"He's as stubborn as you are. But if I could tell him you'd changed your mind—"

"Let's wait and see what Sykes has to say," Maitland suggested. "Would you like us to see him downstairs, Uncle Nick, or would you prefer to sit in on our discussion?"

"I have a great regard for Chief Inspector Sykes," said Sir Nicholas. "Besides, I must admit to a certain amount of curiosity as to what you have to say to him." Which seemed to answer the query well enough. "Meanwhile," he added, "have there been any fresh developments?"

"Nothing but a report from Cobbold's," Horton volunteered. "A few additional items on William Stoddard, not very significant, I think."

"You never told me," Antony said reproachfully.

"There hasn't been time. I picked it up when I went to the office to sign my letters. They say he's well thought of by his company, has lots of friends, few intimates. The people in the shop below are only there until seven o'clock . . . quite frequently see young ladies arriving . . . no idea, of course, how long they stay. People in the flat above say entertaining often goes on till late; they'll hear the murmur of voices or a snatch of music as they pass the front door. No rowdiness . . . no idea whether there's one person concerned, or a dozen. Leaves us, in short, exactly where we were."

"Discouraging," Antony agreed, and looked at his uncle in a deprecating way.

"The only other thing is that Stoddard's parents are reported to be in deep water financially. At least, there are unpaid bills, and they're still driving a 1960 car, though they always used to change every two years."

"I don't see how that fits in."

"Nor do I. I'm just telling you."

Sykes arrived then, and there was an interval during which he was provided with coffee and a sugar-basin to himself. He sat in the chair at the opposite side of the hearth to Sir Nicholas, and looked like a farmer who had just put through a successful deal. He was perfectly at ease—Maitland could hardly remember ever having seen him ruffled—and the proprieties must be observed, the polite inquiries as to everybody's health, the concern over Horton's adventure. Then he looked up at Antony, who had taken his favorite stance with one shoulder propped against the mantel and his back to the empty grate, and said seriously, "I could have told you, you know, that it wasn't any good. With someone else Inspector Conway might have been happy to cooperate. But not with you, Mr. Maitland, not with you."

"So I discovered."

"He is under no obligation to do so," Sykes pointed out.

"I suppose he thought there was a trick in it somewhere." He was talking at random, not really interested now. "Some way I could have thrown doubts on the identification. I don't know what."

"Well, now, Mr. Maitland—"

"If I could see exactly how it could be worked, I might be tempted to try it," Antony admitted. "But now I'm asking for *your* help, and that, I hope, is something else again."

"I don't quite see—"

"No deception. Nothing up my sleeve. Something you could do for me, Chief Inspector, if you would."

"You understand, I have no connection with the case. Superintendent Forrester wouldn't thank me for interfering, to say nothing of upsetting Inspector Conway all over again."

"Nothing like that. Nothing to do with this case at all . . . on the face of it."

"You're going to have to explain it to me, lad," said Sykes good-humoredly. "At the moment I'm fair flummoxed."

"All right, then. Will you tell him our line of defense, Geoffrey?"

"If you like. If you can call it a defense." In spite of his misgivings, he gave, Antony thought, a pretty good account, both condensed and clear. When he had finished, Sykes was looking puzzled.

"You don't sound very sure of yourself, Mr. Horton, if you'll forgive my saying so."

"I don't care for coincidences, so I'm inclined to believe in Langton's innocence since the attack on me," said Horton carefully. "But I'm not sure of the wisdom of telling this story in court."

"That doesn't surprise me."

"It's the only answer we've got to the question about the money," Antony protested.

"Even so—"

"Wait a bit! Let's see where it takes us. Langton was framed; therefore, somebody knew his circumstances and deliberately planted Molly Browne in Oakhurst as an accessory. That's quite simple—"

"It requires a rather comprehensive act of faith," said Sir Nicholas.

"So it does, but we've got over that bit. I was going to say, there's no great difficulty there. The scene is set, Molly Browne comes to Oakhurst, in due course the murder is committed, and the pair of them have Langton just where they want him. But two mysteries remain—"

"Only two?"

"For the purposes of this argument. One is, why was Molly Browne killed a year later? And the other, where was she during the three years after she left home? And during the period after she left Oakhurst too, of course. The first isn't really important; I'd hazard a guess and say her partner grew tired of her charms. The second is absolutely vital, and I think I've got the answer." He paused; then, looking around to make sure they were all listening: "I think the murder of Ruth Langton wasn't an isolated affair. I think we shall find, if we trace Molly Browne's activities, that the same game has been played before . . . perhaps more than once."

"No, really, Antony, we're getting to the borderline of insanity now," Sir Nicholas protested. Horton compressed his lips as though he didn't like what had been said, but Sykes was nodding to himself.

"I'm not at all sure, Sir Nicholas, that there mightn't be something in it," he said. "It's a recognizable pattern . . . the same scene played over and over again. Think of George Joseph Smith, think of George Chapman, think of Haigh, for that matter." He paused, ruminating. "Of course, we're a long way from proving it," he said then, his native caution reasserting itself. "I'm just saying it might be true."

"It was an odd arrangement, wasn't it?" said Horton, "with Molly doing all the spadework, as it were, and her partner just turning up at the critical moment."

"I suppose they took a holiday together sometimes. Otherwise, the game would hardly be worth the candle."

"I wonder where they went."

"Brightsea, perhaps. It seems to keep cropping up."

"Perhaps so. But if it is all true," said Geoffrey, returning to the point from which he had digressed, "I don't see how it helps us."

"It would take the heat off Langton, wouldn't it, if we could show it was just part of a larger plot?"

"Not really. You're postulating a sort of one-man Murder Incorporated—well, one man and one woman, if you must be precise—but isn't it much more likely that Molly Browne and her partner worked to order?"

"Much more likely," said Sir Nicholas, with more emphasis than was strictly necessary. Antony ran his fingers through his hair.

"All the same, I think we must try to find the other man," he said.

"Langton's accomplice . . . who else?" said his uncle bluntly.

"I don't believe that, sir."

"That is not the point at issue."

He paused, and Sykes said into the brief silence, without any effect of haste, "How are you going to set about it, Mr. Maitland?"

"That's where you come in, Chief Inspector. You could get the details—couldn't you?—of unsolved murder cases during the last three or four years."

"And when I've done so?"

"We see which ones fit the pattern, and investigate those."

"I see." Sykes sounded compliant, but there was a degree of dryness in his tone. "Er—when did you say the case was coming on?"

"Not before the end of the week," said Antony, grinning. "Probably not until next week, if we're lucky."

"Quite a program; isn't it?"

"Yes, but we haven't much choice. I could tell you where to concentrate," he added persuasively. "Brightsea, and Scarborough, and Keswick in the Lake District. Those are all places Molly Browne displayed some knowledge of; that might give us a lead."

"Inspector Conway has already circulated a copy of her photograph in the *Police Gazette*; there may be some information from that quarter too."

"So he isn't quite so unconcerned as he tries to pretend."

"He's a conscientious officer."

"Yes, but I wish his conscience didn't make him quite so prickly."

"And if we do find a case, or cases, that fit the pattern—?" said Sykes.

"I know what you're going to say. Molly's partner may be anyone . . . even someone we've never met."

"I'm sure you've thought of that for yourself, Mr. Maitland."

"All the same, I'd like to try. You've listened to me very patiently, Chief Inspector—"

"'Appen I'll find more to try my patience before we're through," said Sykes in a resigned tone.

And Sir Nicholas, who had been listening in silence, laughed suddenly and said; "You're a brave man, Chief Inspector."

"Kind," said Jenny, and filled his coffee cup until it was almost overflowing.

Antony and Geoffrey looked at one another. It would have been hard in that moment to know which of them was the more uneasy.

Part Three

Regina versus Langton

1965

Thursday, the Second Day of the Trial

He wasn't even curious any longer, though once it had seemed so important. He was used to the unsolved riddle of Ruth's death, of course; but who had killed Molly Browne, and why—above all, *why*?—had she been brought back to Oakhurst to lie in the grave among the laurels, not twenty yards from his house? Now it no longer seemed to matter; perhaps he was too tired to care. Even the thought of Susan did nothing to rouse him from his apathy, though at first his mind had turned to her with an almost sick longing. She was part of that other, busy life, that now he felt must have been lived by someone else . . . not, surely, by Henry Langton, who had been in prison for eight weeks, or for an eternity, and who had listened yesterday—after an agonizing wait that lasted into the late afternoon—to an indictment which cited against him two charges of murder.

Vaguely he was aware that this lethargy was unsatisfactory, that anything would have been preferable . . . pain, or loneliness, or fear. He had cause enough for the latter, or so it would seem, but that didn't seem to signify either. He looked out across the court: at the judge, who looked like a cherub, but in whom he had already observed a caustic humor; at the jury—a seedy bunch, he thought them, to hold his fate in their hands; at the lawyers, and the clerks, and the newsmen, avid for sensation, and the spectators, to whom he supposed the trial represented Drama, or perhaps no more than "a nice change."

Perhaps if he could have seen Maitland again . . . he stopped there to examine the thought, and found it an odd one, because he couldn't feel at ease with counsel as he did with Geoffrey Horton; and that was odd, too, when Horton almost certainly believed him guilty, while there was at least a fifty-fifty chance that Maitland didn't.

There they were now: Maitland and the tall, thin man who was acting as his junior—Stringer, wasn't it? Some name like that—and the solicitor sitting behind them and looking far more tense than either. Stringer was writing, but Maitland was sitting very still; he might be taking in every word that was being said, or he might be rapt away to somewhere far from the courtroom; there was simply no telling. Langton found him enigmatic, and disliked the feeling, but at the same time he knew with uncomfortable certainty that if he had any hope at all, it was with Maitland that it lay.

There was the Crown counsel, too; and perhaps he is even more important in my affairs, thought Langton, turning his head until Sir Gerald Lamb came into view. A scholarly-looking man, with pince-nez perched on an aristocratic nose; and he had an odd way of carrying himself, so that he reminded you of a large, sad bird, shoulders hunched against the wind. Not that the slightest breeze stirred in the courtroom; the judge had made it clear at the very beginning of the proceedings that he would not tolerate drafts. Lamb had opened the case for the prosecution as though the contemplation of the villainy he was outlining was almost too much for his spirits, as though it filled him with despair; but for all that, he hadn't minced matters. A deadly recital it had sounded, and what had the defense to offer in refutation, after all? A story of which Maitland had at first said firmly, "we can't risk it" . . . come to think of it, what had made him change his mind?

Mr. Justice Conroy thought that if the prosecution could prove one-half of the facts Sir Gerald had mentioned in his opening, the defense would find itself at a standstill. There was Maitland's habit, of course, of attacking in an unexpected quarter—confident of his ability to control the court, his lordship looked upon the charge of unorthodoxy with a calm if not an indulgent eye—but on this occasion it was hard to see where counsel for the defense would find the opportunity of exercising his talents.

So far there had been no chance of judging what line they intended to take. The evidence of identification had gone unchallenged, as was to be expected . . . so far as concerned Mrs. Ruth Langton, that was. The other case was more complicated. The constable from Oakhurst who had accompanied the body to the mortuary had given his account, and the pathologist who had performed the examination in his presence, and the dental surgeon who had been later called in; but now they were calling for Mathilda Jane Armstrong, who might be hoped to have something more interesting to say, who might even tempt Maitland out of his silence.

Mrs. Armstrong was plump and tearful, as unlike as possible to her daughter Cathie. She accompanied counsel for the prosecution through the preliminaries with no more than an occasional sniffle, but had to stop to wipe her eyes when he led her into the mortuary. (A witness after Lamb's own heart, thought Maitland, who had been depressed himself, but now, perversely, cheered up a little.) Yes, indeed, she had been able to identify her daughter Mary. She had an appendix scar, but it wasn't just that. The birthmark, she'd never seen one just like it, so when they showed her, of course she knew at once. And then later they had told her that the dentist had confirmed . . .

"Yes, well, thank you, madam, no need to go into that

now," sighed Lamb, as sadly as if there was no hope for either of them, in this world or the next. "Perhaps if you would just tell us when last you saw your daughter."

"Four years ago, it would be. Four years in January."

"And you have not seen her since that time?"

"Not once."

"Or heard from her?"

"Only that Cathie had a postcard. My youngest daughter, that is. It didn't say where she was staying."

"I see." Lamb pondered that a moment, gloomily. "Now, madam, I should like you to look at this photograph—which, with your lordship's permission, I shall be putting in evidence—and tell us if you recognize it."

"Well, I ought to, oughtn't I, seeing it's the one I gave that inspector who came?"

"Just as a matter of form," urged Lamb, in despair.

"Then . . . yes . . . it's my daughter, Mary. Molly, the young people used to call her, but Mary was her proper name."

It was a professional portrait, carefully posed. Not as attractive as the missing snapshot, Maitland thought, but a nice-looking girl, for all that. "Would you say it was a good likeness?" Lamb was asking.

"Oh, yes, very good."

"Thank you, madam. I have no more questions."

Maitland himself rose to cross-examine, and felt rather than heard Geoffrey's sigh of exasperation behind him. Perhaps Horton was right, after all; he should just let it go. . . . "How old would Mary have been now, if she had lived?"

"She'd have been twenty-nine at Christmas."

"Was she married?"

"No."

"Engaged to be married, perhaps?"

"Not that either. I sometimes thought she had too many friends," said Mrs. Armstrong, encouraged by counsel's casual manner, and settling herself in the obvious anticipation of a good gossip. "It wasn't easy for her to make up her mind."

"Have you any reason to suppose she got married after she left home?"

"Well, from what I've been told—"

"From your own knowledge, Mrs. Armstrong." He smiled at her. "I'm not allowed to ask you anything else."

"Only that I can't see any other reason why she should have gone, unless there was some man behind it," said the witness darkly. "Not that I'd have stood in her way, you know . . . it was high time she was thinking of settling down, and so I told her."

"So you wouldn't have been surprised to hear—"

"Not surprised, no. But she'd no call to go about it in that underhand way."

"There had been no disagreement between you?"

"She knew I wouldn't stand any nonsense. All the same, she was a good girl."

Maitland couldn't quite bring himself to the agreement that seemed to be expected. "To return for a moment to the photograph that my friend has introduced into evidence, before you gave it to the police inspector, where did you keep it?"

"Well, it was in the bureau drawer."

"But it is framed and mounted. Why didn't you keep it in view?"

"Well—" said the witness again.

"You were ashamed of your daughter, perhaps."

"Nothing like that. You've no right to suggest—"

"If you would explain your reasons to me, I should have no reason to suggest anything, Mrs. Armstrong. You have said it was a good likeness," he added encouragingly.

"And so it was. But it was too—too quiet for Mary. She was always on the go."

"A misleading portrait, then?"

"Not at all. Anyone would know it was Mary."

"Even though you thought it so bad you kept it in a drawer. I see."

"No, I—"

"Tell me about her friends. Was there anyone in particular—?"

She seemed glad enough to leave the subject of the photograph. "There was a very nice steady boy called Ashley . . . Horace Ashley. I'd have been glad to see her marry him. Or Tom Kinglake, but I don't really think they were suited."

"No one else?"

"No one special. She had lots of friends."

"Now, when she went away . . . you're sure she went of her own free will?"

"I never thought anything else. She packed her suitcases, you know—well, one of them was mine, if everyone had their own, not that I grudged it her—and took all her newest things."

"Had she ever spoken to you of any ambition . . . any way of life she'd set her heart on?"

"She liked nice things. Most girls do," she confided. "I daresay she'd have liked to marry a millionaire."

"But there would have been no reason for her to leave home to do that? Or, indeed, to marry anyone at all."

"I'd have been glad to see her married. She knew that."

"But not, perhaps, to see her form some less regular connection."

"Well, really!" said Mrs. Armstrong, outraged, while Sir Gerald Lamb moaned, "My lord!" in heartbroken tones.

"I'm sorry—I'm really very sorry, madam," added Conroy in parenthesis to the witness, "but I do not feel that in the circumstances the question is unreasonable."

"She was always a good girl," said Mrs. Armstrong, having recourse to the handkerchief again.

"As long as she lived at home you would not, of course, have tolerated anything else," suggested Maitland unfairly.

"No, I wouldn't."

"And there had, in fact, been no argument between you, no disagreement."

"None at all. Well, only if I didn't like one of her friends, I'd tell her that."

"How often had that happened?"

"Once or twice."

"Recently? Within a few months, say, of the time she left home?"

"My lord, I do not see the point of this line of questioning," said Lamb, more in sorrow than in anger.

"I confess, Mr. Maitland, I am not quite clear myself as to its relevance."

"The character of the deceased, my lord—"

"Well, perhaps." He sounded hesitant, and Maitland turned back to the witness in something of a hurry.

"Some friendship you didn't approve of, Mrs. Armstrong. Can you help me?"

"There was a young man I thought was fast. Bill Stoddard—"

"My lord!"

"—I didn't think he was doing Mary any good."

"Thank you very much, Mrs. Armstrong. Thank you very much indeed."

Lamb, balked of his protest by his opponent's swift withdrawal, did not wish to reexamine.

But there remained the photograph which had been admitted to evidence, and the next thing was to get it sworn to as a likeness of Molly Brown, which was done by her nearest neighbor at Rose Cottage and by the grocer's assistant, Mrs. Plackett, who also described the handbag the dead woman usually carried . . . though not without interruption from the defense. Counsel for the prosecution relaxed visibly when they went back to the expert witnesses, and his opponent retired into his shell again, leaving Stringer to employ whatever harassing tactics he had a mind to. The pathologists; the photographers; the fingerprint men, who had found nothing of moment in the room where Ruth Langton had died, nothing that couldn't be accounted for. ("This is a complicated matter," counsel for the prosecution had warned in his opening, "and it may not be immediately obvious to you how the two cases are connected." But now, surely, it was clear enough; when Lamb decided to underline a point, he underlined it.) The man who had drawn the plan of Dr. Langton's house and garden; the laboratory experts . . . and here, again, the emphasis was on the second murder, and the court could be in no doubt at all that Maitland was awake. The degree to which the clothing had rotted, the amount of protection it provided when decomposition took place, how long had Molly Browne lain there? How long? The argument carried them on through the long hours of the afternoon, and was inconclusive at last. Nothing to say the defense were wrong in their estimate . . . nothing at all to prove they were right.

That ought to have been that, and quite enough for one day, as Maitland admitted ruefully to Derek Stringer as they left the court. They halted in the doorway, waiting for Horton to collect his papers and join them, and Stringer asked, "These inquiries of yours. How are they going?"

"We're getting nowhere, fast."

"We need something, you know."

"Of course I do. Otherwise—"

"We can't use that cock-and-bull story without some confirmation, Antony."

"What choice do we have? Geoffrey has spoken to Langton—"

"I know. He's adamant!"

"Well, he is."

"And this story about the handbag isn't going to help matters. It was bad enough when he denied having seen it, but this tale of finding an envelope addressed to Molly Browne inside, and thinking it was a sort of warning that another blackmail demand was coming up—"

"I think that's quite reasonable."

"If he hadn't destroyed it."

"To be exact, Derek, he threw it over Putney Bridge one night when no one was around."

"What did he want to do that for?"

"To get it out of his wife's way, I suppose."

"And another thing," said Derek bluntly, "the jury won't believe Molly Browne was a tart just because you suggest it to them."

"If they did, it wouldn't help." He broke off to smile

at Horton as he came up to them. "I'm seeing Sykes again tonight," he said. "There may be something. . . ."

/ 2 /

Sykes was awaiting him in Brackett's, a favorite resort . . . a basement café not far from Scotland Yard. It was cool there today . . . cooler than the streets, and certainly cooler than the courtroom. Antony relaxed, and accepted a cup of tea with gratitude.

"Tell me, Mr. Maitland," said Sykes, stirring in sugar with gentle persistence, "has Inspector Conway given his evidence yet?"

"Not yet."

"He isn't pleased with us, you know," said Sykes placidly. "He isn't pleased with us at all."

"I suppose he's quite aware of what you're doing."

"Oh, yes. I cleared it with him, and with Superintendent Forrester too. As for the inquiry, I'm not saying it isn't interesting, *and* instructive; you'd be surprised some of the odd cases I've turned up. But nothing that will really help you, Mr. Maitland. Nothing, so far."

"You've put out a general inquiry, then?"

"That's right. And it takes time; you'll understand that. Mind you, I asked the places you mentioned to take special care, but I don't think you're going to be pleased with their reports."

"Tell me the worst," said Antony, and helped himself to buttered toast.

"A couple of intriguing cases from Brightsea—I really ought to read the *Gazette* more carefully—but neither of them has any points of similarity with this business you're worrying about, and the local police are positive they never saw Molly Browne before. Scarborough's the same; I thought at first I'd stumbled on something there, but it turned out the suspect had been in a pub and had a whole host of witnesses to his alibi. I won't weary you with all the information that has come in; there's nothing relevant.

And I'm beginning to think, Mr. Maitland, that you're on the wrong track, after all."

"Nothing from Keswick?"

"Not yet."

"I see."

"But there is one rather odd case from Hutton Caldbeck, which is in the Lake District too. Would you be interested in that?"

"Anything . . . anything!"

"Young wife, elderly husband, money in the background, as you might expect. She seemed genuinely fond of him, I'm told, heartbroken when he died."

"How did he die?"

"Strangled with his own scarf while she was at the pictures with a friend."

"But that's almost an exact parallel."

"Almost," Sykes agreed.

"Well? What was the friend's name?"

"Bridges. She was a widow. But—this is where the difference comes in—she stayed at the local hotel, so she never had to give a banker's reference. Nobody visited her . . . nobody wrote to her, even . . . all the time she was there."

"Even so, I'd better get Geoffrey to go to the Lakes with me for the weekend."

"As to that . . . no need, perhaps, to worry Mr. Horton."

"What do you mean?"

"The Assistant Commissioner has given instructions—"

"How on earth did *he* get into the act?"

"Perhaps he feels we owe you a favor, Mr. Maitland. Perhaps he just wants to get the matter cleared up, one way or the other. He says you are to be accorded every facility, but there is a proviso, I'm afraid."

"What is it?"

"That Inspector Conway accompanies you."

"Oh, no!"

"It's quite reasonable, really," Sykes pointed out. "If there's anything in this idea of yours—"

"Reasonable or not, it's a frightful bore."

"I wouldn't say that."

"What would you say then?"

"Stimulating, perhaps. In any case, it's high time you learned to appreciate him."

Maitland laughed. "Not the other way around?"

"On the whole I should say Inspector Conway has an excellent appreciation of your qualities," said Sykes dryly.

"I don't altogether like the sound of that. However . . . is he resigned to giving up his weekend?"

"More or less."

"And if there's any further information, he'll let me know?"

"That's the idea. Mr. Maitland—"

"Yes?"

"Are you sure you know what you're doing?"

"I know what I'm trying to do."

"It's like Sir Nicholas said the other night," Sykes persisted. "I've got an open mind about this business; that is, I'm quite prepared to believe that this Murder Incorporated may exist. If it exists, presumably the fact is capable of proof, but how will that help your client? It's so much more likely that he hired himself a killer . . . the fact that you don't believe it doesn't necessarily make it untrue."

"I know that. Do you think I haven't thought about it? But what choice have I now? I've started the wheels turning . . . you won't drop the investigation, Chief Inspector, no matter what I decide to do?"

"No," said Sykes, and waited.

"This way, at least I shall know the worst. And I suppose I'm hoping that something will turn up. I don't want Henry Langton to be convicted, Chief Inspector. But even if he's acquitted and there's any doubt about the acquittal" —he paused, and drank the last of his tea—"let's not think about that."

"Very well," said Sykes equably. But the thought crossed his mind that for the last few days at least his companion had thought of little else.

Friday, the Third Day

Somehow he hadn't been quite prepared for Mrs. Jackson's attitude, though he remembered that Susan had warned him the housekeeper was spiteful. There had passed without incident—without incident, but with what deadly effect—the testimony of Ruth Langton's doctor and solicitor; of the agent who had rented Rose Cottage to Molly Browne, and the representative of the bank which had held her deposit for long enough to give a reference; of Henry Langton's banker, too. At any other time Maitland would have found some amusement in watching the effect of this last-mentioned evidence. Trust an unimpressionable British jury to have their attention roused by the mention of hard cash. But his talk with Sykes seemed to have clarified his fears, and in so doing intensified them, so that they were at the forefront of his mind, leaving no room for idle thoughts.

Now here was the housekeeper in the witness box, stout, gray-haired, and self-complacent, taking the oath in a slightly affronted tone. She answered Lamb's questions with an eagerness which she did not even trouble to conceal. "I lived at Oak Dene ever since Miss Ruth was married . . . 1957 that would be . . . June, 1957. Of course, there wasn't so much to be done in those days, but what I went through after she became ill, I couldn't begin to tell you."

"I think we understand that, Mrs. Jackson," said Lamb in heartbroken tones.

"Yes, well, it wasn't just that there were things to do for her, you know, but along of the doctor being so untidy. Supposed to be absentminded—that's what *she* said—but I think it's just carelessness. Yes, of course I remember the day she died; a Wednesday it was, my day off, when I always go up to town."

"Dr. and Mrs. Langton were entertaining?"

"They were. He'd forgotten, you see, that I wouldn't be there to look after things. And all the glasses still in the drawing room when I got back, not but what she'd have cleared them, poor lady, if she hadn't been killed."

"You came home late, I believe."

"On the last bus. I always caught that on a Wednesday. I'd have a bit of supper after the pictures, and then it was just convenient. She was dead by then, of course, and the police in the house, and I don't suppose I shall ever forget the shock it was; so I thought to myself, it won't be long before there's a new mistress here, and I wondered whether I'd make a change, but then I thought perhaps I wouldn't."

"Had you anybody particular in mind, Mrs. Jackson?" asked Lamb, with a sigh for the inconstancy of human nature.

"Why, that Miss Desmond. Miss Susan Desmond. Her that's Mrs. Henry Langton now."

"You had some reason for thinking the doctor wished to marry her?" (Derek Stringer was getting restless, but Maitland was undecided; an objection would have a good chance of succeeding, but on the whole, it might be better to let her air her spite. . . .)

"I knew what I'd seen," the witness was saying. "He was making up to her, and in his own house, too. I wasn't the only one . . . and I was right, wasn't I? Six months, and he was courting her; and at the end of the year, they were married."

"Yes. Quite."

"Which you might say was to be expected, seeing him and Miss Ruth had had separate rooms for so long. Not that I think that was an excuse, for a nicer woman never lived."

"Thank you, Mrs. Jackson." He might be grateful for the information; it didn't seem to make him any happier. "Now, before Dr. Langton remarried, can you tell me the routine for dealing with sick calls at night?"

"Yes, of course." Maitland's attention wandered; he'd heard all this already from Ian Bannister, and it was obvious enough that the doctor could have gone out of the house on any one of a dozen occasions, without Mrs. Jackson being any the wiser. All very well to maintain that Molly Browne had come to her grave in the shrubbery while the house was empty and Henry and Susan on their honeymoon; there was no proving it, any more than the housekeeper could prove her innuendos, but there was no doubt at all who the jury would believe. "—so you see, if the phone had rung in my room, I'd just have thought the doctor had gone out already on a call."

"Thank you. That is very clear. Now we must turn to the blind cord in Dr. Langton's surgery. Can you tell us when first you noticed that this had been cut away?"

"Not until the police came looking for what had killed that poor young thing."

"It might have been cut a few days earlier, or several weeks perhaps?"

"With respect, my lord—!"

"Yes, Mr. Maitland?"

"If my friend is to recite all the possibilities—"

"I think perhaps your question might have been better worded, Sir Gerald," said Mr. Justice Conroy, who prided himself on his impartiality.

Lamb gave a moan, and proceeded to take the longer route to his destination. "Was the blind often used in the surgery?"

"Not ever."

"During—say—the three months prior to the discovery of Mrs. Browne's body, did you at any time have occasion to raise or lower the blind?"

"What would I be doing that for?"

"I don't know, madam. I am just asking you—" The effort seemed almost too much for him.

"Well, I didn't."

"And so you did not observe that the cord had been cut."

"No."

"Were you surprised afterwards? Did you say to yourself, it's funny I never noticed?"

"Nothing like that. Because it wasn't, you see." She paused, and added, before anyone could stop her, "It was different for him. He was working there every day."

"My lord!"

"You would like the witness to amplify that remark, Mr. Maitland?" asked Conroy courteously.

"No, I—" (The old blighter knew perfectly well. . . .)

"I think perhaps the freedom with which the witness is allowed to express herself leaves something to be desired, Sir Gerald," said the judge, proving that he had, indeed, known. Lamb looked up at him with sad eyes.

"As your lordship pleases. Mrs. Jackson, did you at any time notice that one of the accused's handkerchiefs was missing?"

"If I was to spend my time worrying about things like that! Careless . . . I told you, didn't I?"

"Yes, I see. Now, will you think for a moment of the period after Dr. Langton came back from his honeymoon."

"His second honeymoon," said the witness, setting the record straight.

"Quite. They came home on the seventh of March, I believe."

"That's right."

"The seventh of last March, of course. During that period, did you have occasion to take something from one of the drawers in Dr. Langton's surgery?"

"It was more a matter of putting something away. I'd given him the clean towels, and when I saw them, two days later, just laying about on top of the chest of drawers, I pulled open the top drawer and popped them in."

"What was in the drawer?"

"Bits and pieces. Things he should have thrown away. And a lady's handbag, a big shiny thing. Well, I thought it must belong to Mrs. Langton, so I said to her, 'if you're looking for your bag, it's in the doctor's surgery,' and she looked surprised and said—"

"Thank you, Mrs. Jackson. Did it, in fact, belong to Mrs. Langton?"

"That's what I was trying to tell you. She'd never seen it before."

"Did you mention it to Dr. Langton?"

"No, I didn't. But when I took in the towels the next week, it was gone."

"Could you describe it for us, Mrs. Jackson?"

"Black patent leather. Almost square, and flat. Not what I'd like to be seen carrying myself, but smart, I will say that. Very smart."

"And you never saw it again?"

"No."

And that was that, or almost. A dangerous witness . . . an ordinary woman whose thoughts and emotions the jury would feel they could understand. Not much could be done to put matters right, thought Maitland, coming leisurely to his feet.

"You were fond of the first Mrs. Langton, weren't you?"

"Very fond."

"Tell me, then, how she got on with Dr. Langton."

"She always got on with everybody."

"No quarrels? No hard words?"

"Nothing like that."

"In fact, he was always kind to her. Considerate."

"Two-faced," said the witness devastatingly.

"That is something, if you will forgive my saying so, that you are not in a position to know."

"I know what I've seen."

"But still, you stayed in Dr. Langton's employment when his first wife died. And even when he remarried."

"I was used to his ways."

"Better the devil you know—" said counsel sympathetically; and surprisingly, she relaxed and said in an almost friendly tone, "Well . . . men! There's not much to choose between them."

"You don't think much of us, is that it?"

"Not much."

As a finale it was too good to miss. He bundled his gown around him and sat down.

/ 2 /

Inspector Conway's evidence had been left until the end, presumably to coordinate the prosecution's case, to tie the two murders together without shadow of doubt. You had to admit it was neatly done; the story formed satisfactorily a logical whole. Yes, he had been the investigating officer after Mrs. Ruth Langton was strangled, and recalled every detail with a clarity that Maitland could well have done without. In the course of his inquiries, he had interviewed a lady who gave her name as Mrs. Molly Browne, and her status as widow. Her evidence had concerned the whereabouts of Dr. Henry Langton at the time of his wife's death, and had constituted a complete alibi for him. The alibi could not be confirmed from any other source. Yes, he recognized the photograph which had been put into evidence. . . .

Lamb was up to his favorite trick, emphasizing every point, and then reemphasizing it. The courtroom had become almost unbearably hot, and there was nothing to look forward to at the end of the long afternoon, except the journey north on a crowded train with only Inspector Conway's company to relieve the boredom. The detective had been allowed to move on to the second murder now; in the circumstances, he said, it had been natural that he should be called upon to undertake the investigation. He described the secluded position of the grave, the impossibility of identifying the features, the clothes—or what was left of them—the implication that Molly Browne had died on a Tuesday. There were tools in the garden shed, readily to hand, but nothing to show whether they had actually been used or not. Indisputably, the blind cord had again come from within the house; there was also the handkerchief, a man's handkerchief, with the Langtons' laundry mark in one corner. The mark had been blurred, of course, but it had been clutched in the dead woman's hand; no, he couldn't account in any other way for its legibility. He had questioned the housekeeper. . . .

It was tempting to let Derek cross-examine . . . a thankless task. Maitland got to his feet reluctantly. "When Mrs. Langton died, if it hadn't been for the alibi, you would have asked for a warrant—would you not?—for Dr. Langton's arrest?"

Conway compressed his lips, and gave counsel an unfriendly look. "I should certainly have felt justified in recommending such a course of action."

"But as things turned out, he was somewhere else at the time. With Mrs. Molly Browne. Were you easily persuaded of that?"

"I am not quite sure what you mean."

"You made inquiries, I imagine, as to the degree of acquaintanceship that existed between them."

"I did."

"What did you find, Inspector?"

"They had met, but I should say the acquaintance was a very slight one." Conway's voice was cold, precise. "Mrs. Browne had also attended at Dr. Langton's surgery on a couple of occasions to consult him."

"Not the sort of relationship, then, that might have led him to ask her help."

"Not to my knowledge."

"Though your inquiries were extensive, I suppose."

"I think you could say that they were."

"If there had been anything to find, you would expect to have turned it up."

"It is not always possible to be sure about a thing like that."

"Still, you did your best."

"I did," said Conway, stiff with disapproval.

"And came to the conclusion that Molly Browne and Dr. Langton were barely acquainted."

"Not precisely."

"Perhaps you would explain that to us, Inspector."

"I felt there must be a catch in it somewhere," said Conway after a moment's pause . . . devoted, probably, to finding a better phrase.

"I see. You were still convinced of Dr. Langton's guilt."

"I was."

"Against all the evidence?"

"I suppose you could put it that way."

"So when this further crime was discovered, you were only too ready to believe—again—that he was guilty."

"I acted in accordance with the evidence that came to light."

"No rash judgments?"

"I don't think so." But his tone was positive enough.

"It was in accordance with the evidence that you arrested Dr. Langton?"

"Yes."

"Even though Molly Browne had not then been identified."

"That is so."

"On the strength of a pocket handkerchief and a length of blind cord," Maitland suggested, and Conway's reply came with a snap.

"They showed, at least, that he was acquainted with the deceased."

"Do you think so? The house was empty for a week while Dr. Langton was away. Do you remember that?"

"With his second wife. Yes."

"You wouldn't say it was an impregnable fortress."

"No."

"In fact, entry could easily have been obtained through one of the ground-floor windows."

"There were no signs that anyone had got in that way."

"But when you looked, two months had passed, had they not? Besides, you had already made up your mind as to Dr. Langton's guilt."

"I investigated the case as I would have any other."

"But with this bias. I might almost say, this prejudice."

"No less thoroughly for that." He hesitated. "You have heard the expert witnesses—"

"Indeed we have. They were thorough too?"

"Certainly."

"But in spite of all their efforts and yours, you found nothing to connect Dr. Langton directly with the deceased."

"The fact that the murderer came from the house—"

"Had been in the house at some time or other," Maitland corrected him, not quite gently now. Conway shifted his ground.

"The deceased had no hat, or coat, or gloves, or handbag. The handbag, at least, was seen again."

"In its absence, the fact must remain uncertain, at best."

"With the other indications—"

"And this prejudice we spoke of."

"I was not prejudiced. I deny that absolutely." Conway was angry now. An unbiased observer, Maitland thought, would have admired his self-control.

"I'm sure you weren't *consciously* prejudiced, Inspector." That was a bit of pure provocation. "To go back to the first murder," said Maitland before the detective could retort, "the police were alerted by a telephone call, were they not?"

"So I have been told. It was made, of course, to the local station."

"Almost as if somebody wanted the body to be discovered at the first possible moment."

"Almost as if someone were relying on that to create an alibi."

"We are agreed on that point, then."

"Well . . . yes." Conway sounded startled.

"Dr. Langton was safely out of the way, and the murder must be discovered before his return."

"That wasn't precisely what I meant."

"Never mind. We will go on to the inquiries you made about Molly Browne."

"She was a witness, not a suspect." (There he was, on the defensive again.)

"But you didn't like her evidence, did you? You asked her, at least, who she was, where she came from."

"Yes, of course. She said that after her husband's death, she had wanted a change of scene, and gave me an address in Brightsea as the one where she had lived during her married life."

"Did you check on that?"

"I had no occasion to. There was no reason for her to be lying on that point."

And so it went on.

/ 3 /

The court adjourned early. Maitland went back to chambers, and then home to collect a suitcase. He was to meet

Conway at the station in about an hour's time. As he crossed the square, he noticed that there was a car parked outside number five, a neat, smallish Austin, and as he approached, Ian Bannister got out. At the same moment, a man who had been standing near the corner turned, and revealed himself as Tom Kinglake. "Something seems to tell me," said Maitland, as they converged on him, "that Miss Armstrong is visiting my wife."

"I'm waiting to take her home," said Tom aggressively.

"Both of you?" His eyes went from one of them to the other.

"Well, yes," Bannister agreed. He seemed to find some awkwardness in the situation.

"Since I brought her here—"

"I'm quite ready to give you both a lift, of course," said Ian, with no enthusiasm whatever.

"Did you come straight from the court, Mr. Kinglake?" Maitland asked.

"Yes, we did. Someone's got to look after her."

"And I took a chance on finding her. A woman at the house told me she was coming here on her way home," said Ian. "I didn't know, of course . . . still, as I'm here, I think I'll wait."

Antony left them to it.

Cathie was drinking tea with Jenny, but she put down the cup immediately he went in. "I won't keep you," she said. "Mrs. Maitland says you've only got a minute. I wanted to know what the questions meant that you asked Mum."

He reviewed the cross-examination quickly. "I'm not quite sure—"

"The ones about Molly. About her character, you said."

"You shouldn't really be discussing the case with your mother—"

She dismissed that as irrelevant, as perhaps it was. "Well, then, I think you know what I meant," he told her. "You suggested yourself that she might have gone away with a married man."

"But I didn't think you'd really be interested in that. I

didn't think you'd—you'd blacken her character, just for fun."

He smiled at her then. "There's not much fun to be found anywhere in this case," he said. He wondered why she thought he wanted her evidence.

"I suppose you mean, you have a reason. I wish you'd tell me."

"I can't do that." It came to him again that she had loved her sister, and would be hurt by the truth . . . by what he believed to be the truth . . . whether she believed it or not.

"You said if you solved the mystery you'd let me know."

"I'm a long way from that, I'm afraid. But anyway, not just yet, not while the case is still being heard."

"Why not?"

"You're a witness, Cathie. We may want your evidence," he corrected himself quickly. "I can't talk to you about any aspect of the case except that."

"I was afraid it was no use coming, but Tom said I might as well try," she said dejectedly.

"He has been coming to court with you, has he?"

"Yes, and I've been very glad. It's so boring, just sitting in that waiting room, but do you know who's there as well? Bill Stoddard!"

"I do know, as a matter of fact. Like you, he may be called by the defense."

"Yes, and he's not very pleased about it. He says it's putting him behind with his work."

"Dr. Bannister is waiting downstairs for you too."

"I can't see why he should bother, when he says he's so busy," said Cathie in an offhand way, but she did not sound surprised. "It's the school holidays," she added. "That's why Tom has time. I suppose I'd better go, but I do think it's a bore, that you won't tell me."

"I'm sorry," said Antony, and took her to the door. Jenny gave him an odd look when he came back.

"Why didn't you just tell her you don't know?" she asked. And then, almost accusingly, "Antony, does that mean you've got an idea?"

"I always have ideas," said Maitland, which was no more than the truth, though he did not sound as if it gave him much comfort.

"About the case . . . about who really did it," Jenny amplified. "Uncle Nick says you're mad, that it's obvious that Dr. Langton—"

"Perhaps he's right."

"But you just said—"

"*You* said, love. I didn't disagree with you." He looked around the room and sighed. "I wish I didn't have to go . . . and with Inspector Conway, too."

/ 4 /

Inspector Conway sat in a corner of the railway carriage like a well-bred iceberg, and discouraged conversation. On the whole, this was a relief to Antony, who could think his own thoughts under cover of the evening paper; but it was different when they went along to the dining car, where they were placed tête-á-tête at a table for two. They could hardly, he felt, sit in silence throughout the meal, and as he studied the menu he was casting about in his mind for a suitable opening.

Conway, he noticed, was meditating over the menu too, and was careful in the choice of wine. This was something of a surprise to Antony, who had always considered the Inspector to be without human weakness. Encouraged, he said tentatively, "I'm sorry if this trip has upset your plans."

"Thank you, I am quite accustomed to weekend work."

"Yes, I suppose you are." Any attempt to claim a similar devotion to duty would meet, he knew, with an unsympathetic response. "All the same, it was good of you to come."

"I had no choicc," said Conway, arranging the salt and pepper symmetrically on either side of the mustard pot. And added, still not looking at his companion, "Needs must when the devil drives," which immediately reminded Antony of Sergeant Mayhew, that master of the cliché.

"Some people," he said reflectively, "might take that as

a personal slight. I'm more inclined to think it's unkind of you to call the Assistant Commissioner names."

"What I don't see," said Conway, not quite so coolly as before, "is what you think you are going to get out of it."

Maitland shrugged. "Evidence," he said, and sat back to allow the waiter to serve his soup.

"But it doesn't make sense," said Conway, almost pettishly, when they were alone again. "You must have a very poor opinion of Sir Gerald Lamb if you think he can't deal with the suggestion of conspiracy."

"On the contrary, I'm quite sure he could deal with it in five minutes, standing on his head," said Antony, and Conway stiffened at the facetious tone. "I don't like being up against Lamb. Witnesses break down and tell him things, just to cheer him up. As for the suggestion of conspiracy, I'm hoping—don't tell me I'm an optimist—for something more than that."

"What, for instance?"

"Some proof that Langton wasn't a party to the arrangement, I suppose." He paused, and grabbed at his plate as the carriage gave a lurch. "I know it isn't likely, but it is *possible*."

"If you want my opinion—"

"I should be glad to hear it, of course."

"—you won't prove either one thing or the other."

"Don't discourage me, Inspector. You're not altogether a disinterested party yourself, you know." He had honestly forgotten their encounter that afternoon in court.

"If you're saying again that I'm prejudiced—" Conway said hotly. (He ought to have remembered it, of course; a man like the Inspector didn't easily forgive, simply because he couldn't forget.)

"I expect we both are, don't you? I'm hoping for a miracle, if you like. But whether or not I get it, I still think the conspiracy is a fact."

"Anything's possible, I suppose," the detective told him sourly. And added in a grudging way, after a short pause, "Have you been talking to Chief Inspector Sykes?"

"Not since yesterday," said Maitland, who felt this was delicate ground.

"Then you don't know we have another call to make, at Carlington, on the east coast."

"That's good." He saw from Conway's expression that he did not share this opinion, and added hastily, "Can we fit it in?"

"If nothing happens to delay us. I cannot foresee that it should."

"This second case—"

"The murder of a wealthy old lady. I know no more than that. But someone at the local police station," said Conway reluctantly, "recognized the photograph of Molly Browne."

It was obvious that he had no intention of enlarging on the subject. Antony gave it up and concentrated on what remained of his soup. He had a feeling it was going to be a long weekend.

Saturday, the Weekend Recess

They got as far as Lancaster on Friday night, and left early next morning for Hutton Caldbeck, which is north of Keswick, near the head of Bassenthwaite Lake. The holiday season was at its height, and there was plenty of traffic; too much for Conway, who was driving the hired car, and whose temper worsened visibly mile by mile. There was little conversation between them, Maitland being on his best behavior, and the Inspector having wrapped himself in an almost tangible atmosphere of black hatred for the expedition, which made him a decidedly uncomfortable companion.

Keswick provided them with a late lunch, and they

pressed on to Hutton Caldbeck through the afternoon heat. Their destination proved to be a pleasant little town, obviously in its own way a tourist center if the "Bed and breakfast" signs were anything to go by. The police station was down a narrow street with nowhere at all to park, but when they walked back to it, they found that it was deliciously cool inside. The local Inspector, summoned from his garden, was with them within ten minutes of their arrival.

Conway was still inclined to curtness. "A man called Kenneth Dekker was murdered here some time ago. An unsolved case, I think."

"Yes, unfortunately." The local Inspector was a big man, and slow of speech, but he came quickly enough to the point. "He was strangled . . . I understand that's what interests you. We thought it was the wife, but she had an alibi that we couldn't break."

"Our main interest at the moment is in the woman who provided the alibi."

"Mrs. Bridges."

"Could we see her?"

"I'm afraid not. She was living at the hotel, the Caldbeck Arms, but I am told she left there about three or four months after the crime."

"When did all this take place?"

"In 1961." He pulled a notepad toward him. "She registered at the hotel on the eighth of September and stayed there until the eighteenth of April the following year. The murder itself was on the twenty-second of December."

"Not usually a woman's crime, is it . . . strangling?" said Maitland, who had yielded to the temptation to wander, and was standing with his back to the window. The local Inspector looked at him curiously.

"We went into all that at the time. It *is* unusual, but there's nothing to say it can't be done, and quite easily, too. In this case, he was strangled with his own scarf, which was hanging in the hall, from what Mrs. Dekker told us. Anyone could have done it—the front door wasn't locked, and he was confined to a wheelchair—but the thing is, nobody had a motive. Except her."

"What was it?"

"He was old and rich, and she was young and . . . flighty, by what was said."

"One particular man?"

"Yes. She's married him since. He had an alibi, too."

"Connected with hers?"

"No."

"What was it, then?"

"His television set had broken down. He went to a neighbor's flat to watch a program that he particularly wanted to see."

"You've seen the photograph in the *Police Gazette*?" said Conway, with an admonitory glance at Maitland, as though daring him to interrupt again.

"We've all had a look at it, of course, since your inquiry came through. No one seems to remember her all that well. After all, it's four years and more, and though we made inquiries *about* the lady, none of us saw her more than once or twice."

"The subject of the photograph had fair hair," said Antony. "It looked dark in the picture."

"That fits in with what I remember. Still, it's no use saying I can swear to it, because I can't."

"These inquiries you mention—"

"Well, it seemed she wasn't what you'd call intimate with Mrs. Dekker. Just a casual acquaintance, in fact."

"How did they come to be together, then?" Conway, by now, was quite stiff with disapproval. Maitland's manner became deprecating, but he persisted with his questions.

"They'd met over morning coffee," said the local Inspector, "and got talking about a film that was on that they both wanted to see. I suppose it was natural to decide to go to the cinema together."

"Very likely. What did this Mrs. Bridges tell you about herself?"

"She was a widow. Her former address was in Brightsea

. . . 17, Bayview Terrace"—he was consulting his notes again—"but I never had occasion to check up on that."

Conway started to say something, stopped, and then asked instead, "What about her friends?"

"She'd made a number since she came here, none of them very close friends, of course. They couldn't tell us anything about her, from their own knowledge."

"Did anyone come to see her?"

"Not that I know of. They might be able to tell you at the hotel."

"We shall go there next, if you have no objection."

"None in the world." It was no wonder, Antony thought, that he sounded relieved to have brushed through the interview without open conflict. Conway, on his dignity, would have inspired awe in anyone less placidly inclined.

While they were on their way, he took the opportunity to ask the detective what he had been going to say. "About the address," he prompted, when Conway did not immediately reply.

"Just that it is the same one that Molly Browne gave me."

After that their visit to the Caldbeck Arms was something of an anticlimax. The manager thought it might be a photograph of Mrs. Bridges; but then again, after so long, he wasn't really sure. His wife did the cooking, and rarely came into contact with the visitors; she wasn't sure, either. And the receptionist and the two waitresses had none of them been employed there four years ago.

So all that was left was the register, with the sprawling signature "M. Bridges," and the date written in a smaller, neater hand. And the account book which confirmed the duration of her stay.

Maitland was thoughtful as they made their way back to the car, and hardly noticed Conway's quietness as they took the road for Penrith, and Appleby, and thence into Teesdale. They made good time and spent the night at Guisborough, which gave them an easy run to Carlington on Sunday morning.

Sunday, the Weekend Recess

Carlington is one of the least attractive of seaside resorts, having neither the blatant vulgarity of some nor the picturesqueness of others of its kind. Its amusements tend to the staid, and there is little to attract even the most ardent of sightseers.

Mrs. Barton had lodged from April, 1964, to February, 1965, at a boardinghouse which had been named Bide-a-wee by its proud proprietor. "The dates might be important," said Maitland with an apologetic glance at his companion; but Conway, who knew quite enough about him to discount any show of diffidence, looked more austere than ever, though he made no overt protest.

The local Inspector was thin, but he had a round, cheerful face that looked as if it should have belonged to a larger man. He had a file on his desk, and a sheaf of untidy-looking notes on top of it. "She arrived on the fourth of April," he said. "The Saturday after Easter, that was. And she stayed until the last day of February the following year, barring she was away most of July and August, they tell me."

"Twenty-eighth of February," said Maitland, beginning to do some calculations of his own on the back of a tattered envelope. "That must have been a Saturday, too."

"It was."

"Then it fits perfectly!" He was looking at Conway now. "She was killed on the following Tuesday, the second of March, and buried at Oakhurst sometime before the seventh, when the Langtons came home."

"You're assuming rather a lot, Mr. Maitland." Conway had his briefcase open, and now he handed to his colleague the photograph of Molly Browne. "You've identified the picture in the *Gazette,* I know, but this is perhaps a bit clearer."

"It's the same lady, all right, only she was prettier than this. More lively."

"There, I told you," said Maitland unwisely. Conway scowled at him.

"We *may* be able to prove system," he said in a grudging tone, "But who's to say she died straight after she left here? That's the question."

"Well, I am, for one. Think of the alternative. Langton killed her after he came back from his honeymoon, with three other people in the house."

"If he killed her and buried her on a Tuesday, there were only two. And one of them his loving wife, don't forget *that,* Mr. Maitland."

"I'm not forgetting anything." His voice was a little strained. "I still say . . . well, never mind. You'll not deny her habit of being present in a town where a murder was committed, and giving an alibi to the chief suspect as well, is something quite out of the ordinary."

"It needs explaining," said Conway ungraciously. "Perhaps you could tell us," he added to his colleague, "a little more about the murder here."

The local Inspector was only too ready to oblige. "Old Mrs. Weaver was strangled while she was taking her afternoon nap. The twenty-sixth of September it was, another Saturday, and both the maids out until suppertime. The granddaughter was out, too; the old lady wasn't bedridden, you know, no reason why she shouldn't be left."

"How was she strangled?"

"A chiffon scarf, one of those square things that girls put on their heads sometimes. It belonged to Miss Charlotte Weaver, the granddaughter; she said she'd left it on a chair in her room. But when we came to look into things, we found she was the only relative, quite an heiress under the old lady's will. So naturally we wondered."

"Naturally," said Conway, and shot a glance at Maitland, as though daring him to question the inevitability of this.

"But it was all quite clear . . . she hadn't done it," the local Inspector went on. "She went out to lunch, before the maids left, and didn't get home until after one of them got in."

"And was she accounted for the whole of the time?"

"Fully accounted for. She had lunch with this Mrs. Barton we've been talking about, and afterwards they went for a walk along the cliff path—"

"Just the two of them?"

"Yes, they were alone. Of course, there'd be a few people up there, though most of them prefer the beach; but who's to remember two young women among so many?"

"Nobody, I suppose."

"And then they came back and had tea at Bide-a-wee, and stayed talking in the lounge there until nearly six o'clock."

"If I may hazard a guess," said Antony, "the doctors inclined to the view that Mrs. Weaver had been killed in midafternoon, while the two of them were alone together."

"That's right. Well, they could tell pretty well, because they knew exactly when she'd had lunch, you see. Besides, she was a creature of habit, and would have got up and gone downstairs at three-thirty, if she'd been alive. But Mrs. Barton had only known Charlotte Weaver for a month or two; it wasn't in reason she'd have been willing to tell lies for her, not where a murder was involved."

"I'm sure the alibi was quite genuine. I don't think she needed to lie."

"You're saying—aren't you?—that Charlotte hired someone to do the job, and used her friend deliberately—"

"Not quite that. I think Molly—I think your Mrs. Barton was part of the plot; and afterward she blackmailed Charlotte by threatening to deny they had been together at the crucial time. What would you have done if she *had* denied it?"

"Applied for a warrant for Miss Weaver's arrest, of course."

"Of course. But as it was, you had no reasonable grounds for suspicion . . . you never even looked at her bank account."

"No."

"But you don't believe that, do you, Inspector?" Antony turned back to Conway again.

"Not as you've stated it. It seems I must accept that there was a conspiracy, not only in this case, but in the case of Dr. Langton too. But I can't accept the fact that the people who profited from the crimes were innocent . . . that's too much."

"Would you believe it if we questioned Charlotte and she told the same story as Henry Langton has done?"

"No," said Conway, still uncompromising. Then, in an alarmed tone, "We're not going anywhere near her."

"Why not?"

"For one thing, she'd never admit it."

"I don't suppose she would," said Maitland regretfully. "Well, if you won't, you won't. I knew I ought to have brought Horton with me."

"What do you mean?" Conway was uneasy now.

"That we shall have to subpoena her, that's all."

"And ask her . . . she'd never admit it," said Conway again.

"We can but try."

"I've told you before—"

"—even if you prove that there's been a conspiracy, nobody will believe Henry Langton wasn't part of it," Maitland finished for him; but he gave the Inspector rather a puzzled look. "You won't refuse to come with me to Bide-a-wee, will you? I mean, a place with a name like that—"

"Of course I'll come," said Conway abruptly.

The local Inspector, still cheerful, agreed to accompany them.

Bide-a-wee, in spite of its name—which might perhaps be regarded as evidence of eccentricity—showed every sign of being comfortable and well run. This wasn't surprising, once they had met the owner, Mrs. Pitman, who was comfortable herself, and who looked capable. She remembered Mrs. Barton well. . . . "Molly, I used to call her, a dear girl." (And if that doesn't clinch it, even with Conway at his most skeptical—! said Maitland to himself.)

"Well, now, I'm not quite sure what these gentlemen

want," the local Inspector was saying. "I've given them all the details, how long she was with you and that—"

"We shall be grateful for your impressions, Mrs. Pitman," said Conway, forestalling Maitland's question by a split second.

"I think I could say I was fond of her," said Mrs. Pitman judiciously. "Mind you, she liked everything nice, but it isn't everyone who appreciates what you do for them. Such a pity, her husband dying like that."

"She was a widow, was she?"

"Yes, poor thing, and you could tell she felt it. Came here for the change, she said; no use moping about where everything reminded her—"

"Where did she come from?"

"Brightsea; that's in Sussex, isn't it? No, I don't remember the address."

"Seventeen, Bayview Terrace," the local Inspector put in.

"What was her husband's name?" asked Maitland, forgetting the resolution he had just made to stay in the background.

"Jack."

"Was it, though?" He glanced at Conway, and saw the detective frowning. "When she left, did she leave a forwarding address?"

"No, she said she'd let me know when she was settled, but I never heard. She'd be with her friends again, I expect, so I thought maybe I'd hear at Christmas."

"Does that mean she went back to Brightsea?"

"Well, I don't know that she actually said that, but I certainly thought that was what she meant to do."

This time Conway had a group of photographs, which he spread out on the table. "That covers everything, I think," he said, "except the question of identification. Will you look at these, Mrs. Pitman—"

She looked. She picked out unerringly the portrait of Molly Browne. "That's just like her," she said, "only you didn't often see her still like that." They thanked her, and came away.

/ 2 /

They left the hired car at York, and took the train from there. Conway was again inclined to be taciturn, and buried himself in a copy of *Punch* he had bought at the station bookstall. It wasn't until the griminess of their surroundings suggested they were nearing St. Pancras that he put the magazine down and said, "Look here, Mr. Maitland, I'll grant you were right about the system. But do you really mean to call Miss Weaver—of all people—to give evidence?"

"I don't know." He sounded tired now, and uncertain. "You think it would be unwise?"

"Unwise? It would be disastrous!" said Conway frankly. And then, with something of his old impatience coloring his tone, "Don't you understand? The Crown won't object to your calling that evidence . . . it makes your case quite hopeless, instead of almost so."

"I think it's hopeless in any case. Don't you?"

"Well . . . since you ask me, yes. But that doesn't mean to say you should do anything to make it worse."

"That isn't exactly my intention, you know."

"I'm sure your intentions are excellent," said Conway stiffly, and Antony smiled.

"The way to hell . . . you don't need to remind me. But I thought you'd be pleased to see me on my way."

"You are still determined to use your client's statement, as you conveyed it to me?" asked Conway, ignoring this.

"There are two ways of looking at it . . . even if the choice was mine—which it isn't, as it happens—I don't know what I'd decide."

"Do you really think anyone will believe it?"

"It's a fantastic story, all right, which the jury may well find incredible. But there are two things to put in the other side of the scale . . . we've got to explain the five thousand pounds—"

"That shouldn't be beyond your ingenuity."

"—and we've got to think of the Court of Appeal."

"I don't quite see—"

"It would be difficult to change our defense completely, if we found out anything else at a later date."

"So when you lose your case"—only Conway, reflected Antony bitterly, would have said "when" instead of "if"—"when you lose your case, you will still go on with the inquiry."

"Of course I shall. And I'll tell you something else," said Maitland, suddenly very sure of himself, "so will you!"

"I may be instructed to continue."

"That isn't what I meant."

/ 3 /

"But the funny thing is," he said to Sir Nicholas later, "he seemed quite concerned that I should be making an ass of myself."

"He is not," said his uncle thoughtfully, "the only one." He looked with disfavor at the crumpled envelope that Antony had taken out of his pocket, and at which he was staring in a helpless way. It seemed to be covered with figures, but when Sir Nicholas got a closer look, he saw that it was actually a series of dates. "Have you decided," he asked after a moment's silence, "what you are going to do?"

"Call Langton as the only witness, and have the last word."

"It won't do you any good."

"I know that. If things had gone differently . . . but what we've got to offer in confirmation is unconvincing, to say the least." He thrust the envelope back in his pocket and went over to the open window, where he stood looking down into the square. "It sounds like a counsel of despair," he said. "But I'm not through yet."

/ 4 /

That was before dinner. After dinner, Susan Langton arrived before they had even started on their coffee. "I wonder what she wants," said Antony in a complaining tone; but he went downstairs to the study without delay.

She was still composed, but the strain was greater now. She had taken a chair near the fireplace, and Maitland came to stand with his back to the empty grate, looking down at her. "Is there something I can do for you, Mrs. Langton? If it's a query about your husband's defense—"

"It isn't so much a query as a request. And I know I should have gone to Mr. Horton, but I thought—I thought it was you who would decide really what line to take."

"I shall be acting on his instructions," said Maitland with a smile.

"Yes, but . . . will you listen to me anyway, now that I'm here?"

"Of course."

Her hands were straining, one against the other. "It's about that story—about what Henry told you. You can't use that in court, Mr. Maitland. Nobody would believe it."

"I'm afraid I have no choice in the matter. Even if your husband's wishes were not quite clear, there is still the matter of the five thousand pounds paid to Molly Browne to explain."

"I've been thinking about that."

"We can't just ignore it. Even if it means telling the truth." He hadn't meant to sound sarcastic. He thought she flinched a little from the hardness of his tone.

"Do you think it is the truth?" she asked.

"I—" For anyone else he would have had his answer ready. Now the question came with a bitterness he couldn't mistake. "Yes, I believe him."

"Perhaps you do. The question is whether anyone else will."

She was giving him honesty, at least; he must answer without evasion. "Not unless I can find some confirmation," he told her.

"Then wouldn't it be better . . . I said I'd been thinking about this, Mr. Maitland." She leaned forward, trying to infect him with some of her own eagerness. "The money was paid in cash, wasn't it? Nothing to show it was given to Molly Browne. So he could say he'd had a mistress; nobody would find that strange, knowing about Ruth. And he wanted to pay her off before taking up with me. That's quite reasonable, too. No one would even wonder if he refused to give her name; they'd just think he was being chivalrous." She paused, and only went on when it became obvious that he wasn't going to reply. "At least, he'd have *some* chance of being believed."

"Do you think so?" He seemed to make a deliberate effort to rouse himself. "And what then, Mrs. Langton? Suppose he was acquitted, through telling the court a lie?"

"Better than the truth!" she said; and suddenly she wasn't calm anymore, and her tone was anguished. "Better than the truth!"

"You didn't answer my question. If the jury returns a verdict of Not Guilty . . . what then?"

"I don't want him to be—I don't want him to be convicted."

"Neither do I." He waited, and after a moment she went on, not looking at him now.

"I couldn't live with him again, of course."

"You have less faith in your husband, in fact, than I have."

She made no attempt to answer that directly. "I love him," she said. "But if he did that—"

"Two murders, Mrs. Langton. A woman who trusted him, a girl who was his accomplice. Do you really think he'd be capable—?"

"It happened, didn't it? It happened."

"Somebody killed them," he agreed. "Not your husband." Perversely, he was suddenly quite sure of the truth of what he was saying.

"I wish I could believe that," said Susan, and began to cry.

Maitland looked at her helplessly. "You are making it difficult for me, aren't you? If I could show you . . . if I could prove to you that it was someone else—"

"But . . . can you?"

"I don't know." He spoke slowly, but something in his tone seemed to alert her. She lowered her handkerchief and sat back in her chair with a shamefaced look. "I'm sorry," she said. "I don't know what made me do that."

"You've been too much alone, I suppose. Tell me, Mrs. Langton, have you expressed these—these views of yours to anyone else?"

"Of course I haven't. I won't. Anyway, I don't know what to believe now."

"Try believing what Henry says, for a change."

"But it's so—such a stupid story."

"Stupid or not, we're stuck with it."

"But he was . . . I haven't told you all the truth, Mr. Maitland. He was nervous, all the time after we got back from our honeymoon. When the police came, it almost seemed as though it was a relief."

"Did you ask him why?"

"No. I tried to, but . . . it was all so intangible. I thought I'd just make matters worse."

"I think I can tell you. I think it was because of the handbag."

"But that was such a—such a little thing."

"Not if he recognized it as Molly Browne's . . . which he did. He knew someone had been in the house, of course, but he thought it was a message . . . something to soften him up for the next blackmail demand."

"Oh, no!"

"That's what he says. Again . . . I believe him."

"I shouldn't have come," she said miserably.

"Well, since you are here, may I ask you a rather personal question?"

"If you like."

"When you said just now that you wouldn't go back to your husband, even if he was free, if you believed him to be a murderer . . . was that an easy decision to take?"

"Not easy at all. I'm ashamed to say how difficult it was."

"What I'm wondering . . . do you think a woman might

condone murder, be an accessory in fact, because she was in love?"

"There must be hundreds of cases on record."

"Yes, but I mean, someone quite ordinary, someone you might know and like."

"Someone like Molly Browne? I think she might, quite easily. It would depend on the circumstances, wouldn't it? I know that for my part . . . our emotions make fools of us, Mr. Maitland, I'm afraid."

"Never mind. An easier question now. When Mrs. Jackson saw the handbag in the surgery, did she mention it to you?"

"Yes. She said *my* handbag was in the doctor's drawer. I knew it wasn't mine, of course; mine were upstairs, all present and accounted for. So I asked Henry, and he said it belonged to one of his patients and he'd take it with him when he went on his rounds. I didn't know he was worried about it at all."

"Thank you." Again he thought, it's a good thing we aren't calling her. "Would you like a cup of coffee—or something stronger—before you start for home again?"

"No, I . . . it's good of you, but I don't want anything, thank you."

"Well, just remember . . . if the verdict goes against us, it isn't necessarily the end of everything, you know."

"I'll remember."

"Shall I phone for a cab?"

"Ian brought me. He's outside, in his car."

"I see." He walked with her to the front door. "You haven't confided your doubts to Dr. Bannister, have you?"

"No, he . . . he says he believes Henry. I don't know if that's true, but I couldn't bear to disillusion him."

Ian got out of the car when he saw them at the top of the steps, and came to join them. "All right, Susan?" he asked, but hardly waited for a reply before he turned to Maitland with a question. "Do you still think Cathie Armstrong is in any danger?"

"No, not now."

"I hope you're right. That chap Kinglake seems to think there's something sinister about her having her bag snatched, but the police don't take it seriously. And now she's gone away—"

"Has she, though?"

"To an aunt, or something. Just for the weekend. And he's even infected her family with his alarms. Her mother wouldn't tell me where," said Ian in an injured tone.

"She'll be back tomorrow," said Susan consolingly. "Take me home, and don't worry so."

"If we're to talk about worrying—" Maitland could hear them bickering as they went down the steps and across to the waiting car. What had Ian said? He'd "known Susan forever." But was he really concerned about Cathie Armstrong, or did he just welcome the opportunity to find out what was going on?

/ 5 /

Antony arrived upstairs just in time to take a telephone call from Inspector Conway, who sounded aggrieved. There was a Bayview Road in Brightsea, and a Bayview Street, and even a Bayview Crescent. But Bayview Terrace, where Molly Browne had said she had lived, just didn't exist.

Monday and Tuesday, the Final Days

Monday was a bad day in court. Horton had agreed with something like enthusiasm that the defense should rely solely on the prisoner's evidence; but as Maitland made his opening speech, he was deeply conscious of his own inadequacy. The rest of the day was devoted to Henry Langton's testimony. He made a nervous witness, and was badly mauled in cross-examination, while his counsel drew an odd-looking animal on the back of his brief which a psychologist, if he happened to be of an imaginative turn of mine, might possibly have identified as a wolf in lamb's clothing.

The following day there were the closing speeches, and the judge's summing up, which couldn't be called sympathetic. . . .

. . . And the jury were absent for three hours and forty-five minutes, and came back at last, to return—to the stupefaction of the defense, no less than of the prosecution—a verdict of Not Guilty.

Tuesday, After the Verdict

Stringer informs me," said Sir Nicholas Harding, in a gentle tone that made his nephew immediately uneasy, "that you made a masterly speech for the defense." He was dining with the Maitlands, and had arrived early; purely, Antony felt sure, for the purpose of plaguing him.

"That's nonsense," he said impatiently. "The verdict was completely irrational, and you know it."

"Was it, indeed? I prefer to think of it as a personal triumph for you," said his uncle in a cordial tone. Antony laughed, though still a trifle reluctantly.

"If you *must* ascribe a reason, I should say it was because Lamb couldn't make up his mind."

"What was he uncertain about?"

"Whether Langton was personally responsible for his wife's murder, or whether he used an agent. His cross-examination was most damnably effective, you know. I should think Langton felt as if he was being skinned . . . slowly. But when it came to his final speech, his doubts showed through."

"And you think that was the reason—?"

"My own feeling is that it would have been more effective if he'd come down on one side or the other; but, as I say, I don't think it really made much difference."

"I see." Sir Nicholas sipped his sherry, and spoke in even more dulcet tones. "At least I should have thought you would be gratified by the result."

"Oh, I am!" Maitland was frowning as he spoke. "But I happen to have a weakness for finishing what I've begun."

"What does that mean?" Sir Nicholas wondered.

"That I don't imagine Langton is finding the situation entirely to his liking."

"I don't suppose he is."

"Yes, but I think he's innocent," said Maitland, answering the tone rather than the content of the last remark. "There's another thing, of course. Molly Browne's partner—"

"I thought we should come to him sooner or later. Are the police satisfied that he exists?"

"I don't know. I had a word with Conway after the verdict, but he's on his dignity again. I don't know *what* he thinks."

"I take it there's no question that he accepts Langton's story as it stands. Any more than I do," Sir Nicholas added reflectively.

"Not a hope. I did think at one point he was in two minds about who had killed Molly Browne, but as far as Ruth Langton's death is concerned, I'm pretty sure he thinks her husband is responsible. And that still falls a good way short of what I'd like him to believe."

"I hope you won't mind my saying, Antony, that I think you're being unreasonable."

"I know you do."

"Well, unless Conway intends to take the matter further, I don't see what there is to be done."

"Neither do I . . . now. The trouble with this fellow is that he's elusive. There's no coming to grips with him."

"Why worry? The jury agreed with you."

"Do you think his friends will, too? And his patients?"

"I see what you mean, but it's hardly your affair."

"That's what Geoffrey says. I don't agree with either of you."

"In that case, I must ask you, what do you mean to do?"

"I haven't the faintest idea. If I could think of one thing that would be useful—" He leaned forward to pick up the evening paper that was lying on the sofa, and folded it open with a quick, angry movements at a picture of Cathie Armstrong, arriving home in tears. "I've done well, haven't I?" he asked, thrusting it at his uncle.

"I do not think you can blame yourself that Molly Browne's true character has become common knowledge."

"Perhaps not. The paper says Mrs. Langton was 'unavailable for comment.' What the hell do you suppose that means?"

"Surely she, at least, will be glad—"

"Oh, at first." His tone was savagely scornful. "That was Langton's own reaction . . . relief that it was over. I wonder how long it will take them to realize what they're in for."

"Does he intend to resume his practice?"

"I suppose so."

"I agree with you. I think that would be unwise."

"What else can he do? It's his life." And that was the trouble, of course. But it didn't seem, then, that he could do anything about it.

Part Four

Trinity Term, (continued)

1965

Wednesday, 28th July

Even so, he shouldn't have been surprised to receive a visit from Henry Langton the following week. He came in the evening and was shown straight upstairs by Gibbs, who was in one of his more intolerant moods, though at the best of times he would have preferred martyrdom to using the house telephone which had been installed for his convenience. Jenny had put down her book and prepared to disappear after the first greetings, but Langton said "Don't go!" and sounded as if he meant it, so that she hesitated for a moment, looking at her husband, and then sat down again. Henry took the chair to the left of the fireplace, which had its back to the light, and sat studying his hands; while Maitland stood with his back to the empty grate and leaned one shoulder against the mantel, but looked no more relaxed than the visitor did.

He made no attempt to break the silence, and Langton said at last, as though unwillingly, "It isn't really private, what I've got to say. It's no more than thousands of people must have guessed would happen. Susan's left me."

Something must be said to that, but what use were words

anyway? "I'm sorry," said Maitland inadequately. And Jenny, equally trite, said, "Tell us about it, if you like" . . . because surely that was why he had come. She had never seen Henry before, and thought he looked desperately ill, far more like a man who had been convicted by the jury's verdict than one who had been set free. She was also aware of her husband's uneasiness, as though he had spoken his thoughts aloud.

"At least," said Antony, when the silence had lengthened again almost unbearably, "it's something the press haven't got hold of." Henry laughed, but there was no amusement in his eyes.

"Give them time," he urged. "She only went today." And then, still speaking as though with difficulty, "I told her to go."

The only possible response to that seemed to be, "Why?"

"Because I couldn't stand it. She said she'd stay . . . she didn't want to make it any more awkward for me . . . she didn't want people to talk. She said she'd stay until things settled down again. But everything has gone wrong; some of my old patients have flatly refused to see me, others are impossibly inquisitive. And then to have Susan about the house, and no more to me than a paid housekeeper . . . it wasn't doing her any good either, I can tell you that. So today I told her she'd got to make up her mind. She's gone to her mother's, I think."

"Poor Susan," said Antony, thinking of what Mrs. Harper had told him.

"I'm past caring," Henry went on, unheeding; which was manifestly untrue. "I shall make arrangements to wind up the practice and go abroad, I suppose."

"I see."

"You're wondering why I came here, of course." He paused, as though he found this more difficult than all the rest. "I came because, when you were making your closing speech, I thought you believed what you were saying."

"I did."

"And somehow you made the jury believe it, too. The trouble is"—he smiled again, and this time with something like genuine amusement—"my neighbors weren't there to hear you, and what they've seen in the papers isn't convincing, I'm afraid. It was Susan who told me you have sometimes been able to help people by finding out the truth . . . well, actually, what she said was 'if there was anything to find, he'd have found it.' But I thought you might be willing to have one more try."

"The police are continuing their inquiries in the hope of finding Molly Browne's partner, you know."

"Yes, but . . . look at it this way, Mr. Maitland. Suppose the jury had found me guilty instead."

"We should have gone to the Court of Appeal."

"Well, I have been found guilty, in a way, and there's no appeal from this verdict . . . except the truth."

"I know. I'm sorry," said Maitland again. "You do realize —don't you?—that even if the man who committed the murders is found, people will still think you hired him to kill your wife."

"Yes, I realize that."

"He's not going to be concerned about your happiness. He's unlikely to make a statement exonerating you, for instance."

"I know that too." He moved his hands, as though he were trying for some greater expression than words could give. "I should be thanking you for your trust, not badgering you into doing still more for me. But is it foolish to hope?"

"No, it's . . . if you don't, you might as well be dead." He turned his head to look at Jenny, aware—as probably Langton was not—that the other man had been speaking the more freely for her presence. "What do you think about it, love?"

"I think you should try to help Dr. Langton." But she was answering Antony's need, not the stranger's; and that, too, was something Henry could not know.

"Very well. I'll see Conway again . . . see what—if anything—he's found out." He spoke briskly, hiding his uneasiness from Langton at least. "And there's a woman I'd meant to see, before we got to the Court of Appeal."

"Who is that?"

"Charlotte Weaver. I think it was Charlotte. Her grandmother was murdered, and Molly Browne gave her an alibi too."

"I see," said Langton, but he sounded doubtful.

"I don't know whether she'll talk . . . frankly, I think she'd be a fool if she did. But at least we can try."

When Langton had left them, Antony came back to the living room, and this time he sat on the sofa within reach of Jenny's hand. "It would be terrible," she said after a moment, "to tell anyone not to hope."

"Well, I think so too. But I don't imagine I can do anything for him, love. It may have been more cruel—"

Jenny smiled and moved her hand so that she could return the pressure of his. "You wouldn't be feeling nearly so gloomy if it weren't for having to see Inspector Conway," she told him.

But, "That's all you know about it," said Antony, unconsoled.

Thursday, 29th July

Jenny was so far right, he hated the idea of going to Scotland Yard, but it seemed there was no help for it. He phoned the following morning and arranged to see Inspector Conway at two o'clock that same afternoon.

Last time he had been there, it had been to see one of the superintendents; Conway's room was less imposing, rather a hole-in-the-corner affair really, but perhaps when the impending move was finally accomplished, he would achieve some better accommodation. He had Sergeant

Mayhew in attendance . . . enough in itself to make a far larger room feel crowded.

"I'm sorry to disturb you," said Antony; and Conway replied, "That's quite all right," and contrived to sound as if he didn't mean it. He waved the visitor to a chair and then sat down himself, very erect, while Mayhew lounged beside him. "What can I do for you?" he asked.

"About the Langton case—"

"Haven't you carried your efforts there far enough?" said Conway, at his most unbending.

"I thought we'd agreed to differ about Langton's guilt."

"If you are in good faith about that, we certainly differ," Conway told him.

"Yes, well—" He'd come to ask a favor, hadn't he? No use, then, to lose his temper at the outset. Antony caught Mayhew's eye, and found it amused and indulgent. If he had only the sergeant to deal with . . . "About Molly Browne's partner, Inspector. Or do you think she was working alone?"

"No, of course not. It is obvious that there was somebody else. We have certainly been pursuing our inquiries—"

"Intensive inquiries," said Sergeant Mayhew reassuringly.

"—but I fail to see how that can concern you."

"Because I've got Langton acquitted without proving his innocence," Antony told him.

"I've told you before—"

"Yes, I know. Don't say it again, there's a good chap. If you've been making inquiries, you can surely tell me—" He saw from Conway's expression that the suggestion wasn't a popular one, and changed it obligingly. "Or can't you?"

"We have a much better picture now of their activities," said the detective grudgingly.

"Have you, though?"

Sergeant Mayhew gave a preliminary rumble like a clock about to strike. "Clever," he said with appreciation. "They seem to have worked about one job a year."

"Where? Not in the south of England?"

"How did you know that?" That was Conway, sharp-tongued and distrustful.

"It's part of the pattern," said Antony mildly. "Oakhurst was the exception . . . don't you think?"

"Now, really, Mr. Maitland, you've been doing your best to show system—"

"I only meant . . . how did they set about finding their victims?"

"As a con man does." From his tone, that should have been obvious. "Moving from place to place, if necessary."

"Yes, well, I only meant that I think Oakhurst was a special effort. Somehow or other they knew the Langtons' circumstances, and that made it worth their while to work near home for once."

"Their special knowledge could have come from Langton himself."

"That's true, Mr. Maitland," said Mayhew in regretful chorus.

"Not necessarily," Antony persisted. He saw that Conway was looking skeptical and added as persuasively as he could, "Tell me about the other jobs."

"No harm in that," said the sergeant.

"Well . . . if it will convince you of the futility of your efforts, perhaps it will be time well spent," said Conway, unrelenting. "One was in Colwyn Bay, November, 1962. One in Blackpool, in July of the following year. There's no one in either place will identify the photograph for sure, but the circumstances are identical, I can tell you that."

"No trace of the man?"

"None at all."

"He's either extraordinarily clever, or extraordinarily lucky . . . don't you think?"

"I do."

"If he'd only stop running long enough for us to catch up with him."

"The trouble is, I suppose," said Mayhew unexpectedly, "he probably isn't running at all, he's standing still." It was one of the longest speeches Maitland had ever heard him make.

"That raises another question, doesn't it?" Antony said reflectively. "Where do they go between jobs . . . where did Molly Browne go, at least?"

"It appears she was at Brightsea when she first left home."

"That's just it. All her clues seem to have been false ones. She talked of Scarborough, and did a job at Carlington. She talked of Keswick, and was actually at Hutton Caldbeck. When she mailed that postcard at Brightsea, she was probably really staying at St. Leonards, or Bexhill, or Bognor Regis."

"I don't see how that helps us," said Conway discontentedly.

"It doesn't, does it? Was the Colwyn Bay murder committed on a Saturday?"

"As a matter of fact, it was. You're thinking that the man had some other occupation."

"I expect he had his cover story, don't you?"

"Well, yes, it seems likely. You made a great deal of fuss about Molly Browne's friends in Streatham, Mr. Maitland. Do you think one of them is the man she ran off with?"

"I do, rather. Stoddard lives in Oakhurst now—"

"I'm bound to say, if you really think your client is innocent," said Conway waspishly, "his partner, Dr. Bannister, had by far the best opportunity of killing his wife."

"That had occurred to me."

"In that case, I suppose you want to know when they took their summer holidays in 1963."

"Not really." His casual tone seemed to have the effect of alarming Conway.

"If there is anything that you know, Mr. Maitland, that you haven't told me—"

"Nothing . . . nothing." An idea so nebulous that it would only arouse Conway's skepticism afresh. If there was anything to be gained by frankness . . . but at this stage it might do more harm than good. "Have you any objection to my going to see Miss Weaver, Inspector?"

"I don't see how I can stop you," said Conway ungraciously. "But I can't believe it will do you any good."

"She'll probably throw me out," Maitland agreed, and saw with amusement that this was one course of action, at least, with which the Inspector was in sympathy. "I'd better go," he said.

For some reason Sergeant Mayhew chose to accompany him as far as the entrance on to the embankment. "It's only fair to tell you, Mr. Maitland, that we had no luck with the lady."

"Charlotte Weaver?"

"Yes. It was pretty much as you said. Sent the Inspector away with a flea in his ear, she did. And it isn't good for his temper, you know," he added apologetically, "coming up against a dead end like this."

On reflection, Antony decided that it wasn't altogether good for his temper either. If he could see his way . . .

Saturday, 31st July

This time Jenny drove him. They started on Friday night, speeding north through the dusk and the weekend traffic, and reaching York too late for comfort. "It's a pity we had to delay our holiday," said Antony when they passed the turn they usually took, the one that led to Thorburndale. Jenny said, "Never mind," because it wasn't any good repining, and she knew well enough what Antony would have been like if she'd insisted on going away while all this was on his mind.

Next day they reached Carlington about noon, and had lunch at the Imperial Café, which overlooked the sea. The meal wasn't bad, but there were crumbs on the tablecloth and lipstick on one of the coffee cups. All things considered, they were glad to get outside again and take a look at the town. There was a stiff wind blowing, and not much sun, but there were a few hardy souls in the sea, and the beach was crowded. Antony's appointment wasn't until three o'clock, so they took the cliff path and dawdled along it for a time, while he thought of that other Saturday, only ten months before, when Molly Browne had walked here with her victim while an old lady was killed. Jenny strolled beside him, untroubled by ghosts. He had never been more glad of her presence, nor more apprehensive at the thought of an interview to come.

Charlotte Weaver should have been small and dark . . . rather like Cathie, in fact, except for the color of her hair. He had formed as clear a picture as if he had seen her before, and as so often happened, the reality came as a surprise to him. She was a large, lumpish young woman, badly, expensively, and very unsuitably dressed in tweeds of an uninteresting shade of brown. He hadn't expected her manner to be welcoming, but neither had he expected her to be quite so stiff and ill at ease.

As for the house, it was a period piece. Nothing could have been changed, he thought, since the old lady's death . . . or for long before that. The room in which they sat was over-full of heavy furniture, dark from too-heavy draperies, crowded with knickknacks of every kind. "I believe," he said, casting about in his mind for an opening, "that Detective Inspector Conway visited you recently in connection with your grandmother's death."

"Yes, he did." She sounded sulky. He had to remind himself that he hadn't expected it to be easy. "How did you know that?" she asked; and now there was a touch of sharpness in her tone.

"He told me. Or rather, his colleague did."

"But I thought . . . you said *you* wanted to talk to me about that."

"I'm afraid I do."

"What do you want?"

"A little information, if you'll be kind enough to give it to me."

"Not . . . money?"

"Good lord, no! Nothing like that."

He thought she relaxed a little, though she still looked wary and resentful. "I wondered . . . well, it doesn't matter."

It hadn't occurred to him before that his message might have been misunderstood. "You wondered if I might be connected with Mrs. Barton, shall we say?"

"I don't know what you mean."

"That's a pity, because I was hoping you could tell me—"

"I don't know any more than I told the police," she interrupted quickly.

"Tell me so much then, if you will."

"I don't see what it has to do with you."

"Didn't Inspector Conway tell you that Molly Barton is dead?"

"He said Molly Browne. He said it was the same person. I don't know whether that is true."

"Couldn't you identify the photograph?"

"Oh, that! It was Molly, all right, but I still don't know—"

"What was she like?"

"Well . . . jolly. A bit too full of life, if you know what I mean."

"And yet you became friends."

"That's how she seemed to want it."

"You sound as if that surprised you."

"No. Why should it? We were much of an age, and there aren't too many young people here . . . among the permanent residents, I mean."

"I see. I think I'd better explain to you exactly why I'm here, Miss Weaver. I shouldn't like you to be under any misapprehension about that."

She shrugged. "If that's what you want."

(I don't want to be here at all. Why did I let Langton persuade me?) "I'm a lawyer," he said. "I told you that, didn't I? And I have a client, a doctor, who was recently acquitted of a murder charge."

"I saw that in the papers." For the first time there seemed to be a faint spark of interest in her eye. "I don't remember his name."

"Henry Langton."

"I still don't see what it has to do with me."

"He was indicted on two counts: the murder of his wife, and the murder of Molly Browne. Who is the same person—you could have taken Inspector Conway's word for that—as your Molly Barton."

"Well?"

"Mrs. Langton was killed . . . strangled . . . in February of last year. Dr. Langton had a motive, but at that time it seemed he had no opportunity, because Molly Browne gave him an alibi."

She was sitting very still now, her stare so fixed that it made him uneasy. "What has that to do with me?"

The reiterated phrase grated on his nerves. "Didn't Inspector Conway explain that to you?"

"No, he didn't. He just . . . asked me some questions about Granny's death, and told me about Molly Browne. That's all."

"It had occurred to him, as it has to me, that there is a certain similarity between the two cases . . . yours and Dr. Langton's."

"But everyone knows I couldn't—"

"Molly Browne said you couldn't, and her statement is on record. I don't think you have anything to worry about, you know. It would be a complicated matter to disprove it; and besides, after Dr. Langton's acquittal, it is unlikely that the D.P.P. would recommend a further prosecution."

"I'm not worried." She said that quickly, too quickly. "I don't know what you're talking about, that's all."

"I'm trying to lead up tactfully to the suggestion that there is a further similarity between your case and Dr. Langton's." His own circumlocution both amused and irritated him. "After Mrs. Langton died, Molly Browne threatened to deny he had been with her . . . unless he paid her five thousand pounds."

"Do you expect me to admit that I—?"

"I don't expect it. I hoped, that's all."

"You said he'd been acquitted," she pointed out.

"Unfortunately, he is still suspected by the people who mean most to him, including his wife. They are both bitterly unhappy."

"I can't help that." She paused a moment, and then added, not quite so positively, "Would it do any good if I told you that the same thing happened to me?"

"If you would talk to me, freely, about Molly Browne, I think it might help considerably."

"Well, it's all nonsense, of course. I hadn't any money."

"Not until after probate, perhaps. I understand your reluctance to talk about this, Miss Weaver, but it's only for my private information, you know. There's no question now of your being asked to give evidence, for instance. As you said yourself, Dr. Langton has been acquitted."

"I don't know," she said, sulky again. "Why should I trust you? Even if it was true . . . all this."

"Will you tell me about Molly Browne then, as you knew her?"

"Why should I?"

"Because you've been unhappy and lonely yourself, and you're too kind-hearted to enjoy thinking about other people in the same position."

She seemed to be considering that. For the first time, when she spoke, her voice sounded faintly amused. "I don't think I'm very susceptible to flattery," she said. "What do you want to know?"

"Start with the way you met her."

"It was at a church social. We got talking." Another pause, which he might fill in his own way. "She came here quite a few times after that. Granny liked her; she said she liked a bit of life about the place."

Some resentment there, unless he was mistaken. "But you liked her yourself, didn't you?" he asked.

"She was all right. Company," admitted Charlotte grudgingly. "Well, I saw her at other people's houses sometimes, and when I went shopping; you do, in a small place like this. That's all, really. There's nothing to tell."

"The day your grandmother died—"

"What about it?" She might be completely devoid of feeling, she might be extraordinarily vulnerable, and trying hard to hide it. "I was with Molly . . . you know that."

"At her invitation?"

"If you must know . . . yes."

"How was the arrangement made?"

"By telephone."

"Why that particular day?"

"It was the one she suggested."

"Yes, but . . . a Saturday. When the maids were out."

"It didn't matter. Granny wasn't an invalid, you know. But I might have suggested something else, if Molly hadn't said it was an anniversary."

"What of?"

"I never asked her. I thought perhaps her wedding day, something it made her unhappy to remember, now that her husband was dead."

"Did she speak much of her husband?"

"Not much, I suppose. I told you she was always cheerful. Until that day, and then she said quite a lot."

"What do you know of him, then?"

"Not much. His name was Jack, and he was an accountant, and I think she'd been very fond of him."

"I'm sorry to press the point, Miss Weaver, but you said she spoke of him 'quite a lot.'"

"Yes, but . . . I suppose I mean, indirectly. She didn't say he was tall, and dark, and handsome, and had a sense of humor. She talked about how happy they had been, where they had lived, the things they used to do. She seemed—I don't know whether you're going to believe this, Mr. Maitland—she seemed to *need* to talk about him that day."

"Why shouldn't I believe it?"

"Oh, because . . . you think she was a criminal, practically a murderess."

"Tell me anyway. Where had they lived?"

"At Brightsea. We were walking along the cliff path, and she said it reminded her. She said at Brightsea there was a row of bungalows, not too close together, and theirs was the farthest from the town. You could walk along the path, or go around by the road, by car. She said they used to go out at night and see the moon shining on the water, and the clouds all silvered—"

"Romantic," said Maitland, as she let the sentence trail into silence. She glanced at him suspiciously, but there was no flippancy in his tone, and his expression was perfectly serious. "That's why you won't tell me, isn't it?" he asked. "Because you'd rather remember her like that."

"All right, then, if you will have it. I'd never known anyone like her before," she said defiantly. "She said they were happy, they laughed a lot together. I thought I was being wicked, envying her; and I did envy her, even though she was so unhappy *now*. And then, of course, I realized—" She broke off, and the sullen look came back to her face again. "It's nothing to do with you."

"You realized she hadn't been unhappy at all."

"I was a fool to believe all she told me. I know that."

"I don't know that it was so foolish. I think perhaps you were right, that she needed to tell you, that day; that she needed the reassurance—"

"You don't understand."

"I would try to, if you would tell me."

"Next time I saw her—"

"After your grandmother's death."

"Yes. She came to offer her condolences . . . that's a fine phrase, isn't it? And then she said, 'you do realize, my dear, that this puts you in a difficult position.' And, of course, I didn't realize anything of the sort, because we'd been together. But she said we must be careful to tell exactly the same story to the police."

"I see."

"I don't know why I'm telling you all this," she said, momentarily resentful again. "Don't tell me it's because I'm at all kind-hearted . . . it's something I seem to have to do."

"If you want my assurance—"

"No. I believe you don't want to hurt me. It doesn't seem to matter anymore," she said wearily. "You've guessed the rest of it, haven't you? I said they'd never believe a woman had strangled her, and she told me I was just the sort of woman they could believe it of. She wanted five thousand pounds, and of course I couldn't give it then, but she made me write a sort of promise."

"Wait a bit! When and how was the money paid?"

"To her. Just before Christmas."

"Was probate through so quickly?"

"No, but the solicitors weren't at all difficult about advancing the money."

"Five thousand pounds. I didn't know there was a solicitor living with such a generous nature."

"The way things were left . . . I told them a lie, I'm afraid."

"If you found one they'd believe, that was clever of you."

"No, because . . . Granny left me a letter, you see, asking me to take care of the servants, and her old housekeeper who retired, and the man who came to do the garden, who has an invalid wife. And she specified amounts; it came to six thousand pounds altogether. I don't know why she did it like that, unless she thought it would save legal fees; she got ideas of that sort into her head sometimes."

"So you told the solicitors you were paying these unofficial legacies . . . I see."

"Well, I did pay them really. Only later on."

"Yes, of course." He smiled at her. "I was hoping . . . Molly Browne had a partner, you know."

"I realize that. Do you think it was the husband she talked of? Jack?"

"Yes and no. I think it was the man she talked of, but I don't think that was his name."

"Or even that they were married, I suppose."

"I don't suppose they were. I think they wanted to keep their association very secret."

"But their friends in Brightsea must have known."

"If they were ever there."

"It was all a lie, then. Even that?"

"I think perhaps she described a real place. Not, unfortunately, well enough for me to find it. There's just one other thing, Miss Weaver; have you ever been approached again?"

"No, but I've half-expected—"

"Now that Molly Browne is dead, I don't think *he* will do anything. But if he does, will you promise to let me know?"

"If you like." She was lumpish again, and she gave the assurance unwillingly.

"Don't on any account do anything silly, like paying him," he told her urgently. "Let me know."

"All right, then, I'll remember."

He got to his feet, looked all around the room as though for inspiration, and then back at Charlotte again. "You've made a difficult task easy for me. I'm grateful."

"Even if I didn't help you. I didn't, did I?"

"Not really. No."

"Then I don't see why—"

"It was something I had to do, you see." His smile was disarming. "Even if it didn't do any good."

He was very quiet during the drive back to London. Jenny humored him, and refrained from idle chatter. They got home at about ten o'clock.

/ 2 /

Among the pile of correspondence that Antony picked up as they went through the hall, there was a postcard. Jenny threw her share aside almost as soon as she looked at them; they were mostly end-of-month accounts, and could be dealt with later. But then she found that her husband was still staring at the gaudy picture. "That's queer," he said. "That's very queer."

"What's the matter?"

He made no attempt to answer the question. "Who do we know who's on holiday, love?"

"Dozens of people, I expect. If you want to know who sent the card, wouldn't it be best to look?"

"I . . . yes, I suppose so." He turned it over slowly. "*Wish you were here, Cathie*." he read. And then, with a sudden blaze of excitement, "Jenny, it was posted in Littlebourne."

"But we don't know any . . . I suppose you're still thinking about the Langton case," said Jenny, resigned. "But I can't see why Cathie Armstrong should be sending you postcards. She was pretty well hating you, wasn't she, by the time the trial was over?"

"That's why it must mean something . . . don't you think?"

"What could it mean?"

"A message, if only I could understand it. It might mean just what it says. You see, Jenny, it's the same postcard—the same picture on the card, I mean—as the one Molly Browne sent home. The one that was in Geoffrey's brief-case when it was stolen," he added, with a touch of impatience, seeing her uncomprehending look.

"It is queer, of course." She took the card he was holding out to her, and stood a moment looking down at the garish presentation of "The Promenade at Noon." "But I don't see . . . really, Antony, I don't see what it could mean."

"Molly's card was posted in Brightsea. Everyone thought that must be where she'd gone. But if it was really Littlebourne, and Cathie found out somehow—"

"Why didn't she come and tell you herself? That would be the obvious thing."

"That's what I'm wondering. I don't like it, love; I don't like it at all."

"Well, but—"

"I'm going to telephone." He was decisive suddenly, and moved quickly to the living-room door. "Mrs. Armstrong must be in the telephone book," he said over his shoulder. Jenny followed him with a feeling of helplessness, and found him leafing through the A's. "Here we are . . . Mrs. M. J. Armstrong." He was muttering the number to himself as he crossed to the desk and picked up the receiver. It was with a distinct feeling of anticlimax that he heard the bell shrilling on. "Perhaps she's in bed," he said hopefully. But though he waited and waited, there was no reply.

Inspector Conway was in the phone book too. He rang

him from a sense of duty, and against his better judgment, and wasn't surprised by the lack of cordiality in the detective's tone. "Mr. Maitland? I thought you were going to Carlington."

"We just got back. Inspector, do you know where Cathie Armstrong is?"

"At home in her bed, I should think." It wasn't really as late as all that, but he didn't seem to relish the interruption.

"No, I'm serious. I've just had a postcard from her . . . from Littlebourne; the seaside town in Sussex, not the one near Canterbury."

"It's August, Mr. Maitland. Plenty of people are on holiday."

"It's the same picture—you never saw it, Inspector—it's the same picture that was on the card Molly Browne sent home."

"What of it? They go on selling these things for years and years."

"I tried to ring Mrs. Armstrong," said Antony, in a worried way, "but there was no reply."

"Probably they've *both* gone to Littlebourne," said Conway coldly.

"Yes, I suppose. Will you find out, Inspector?"

"Tomorrow?"

"Yes, I don't suppose there's much we can do tonight."

"If it will prevent you from doing anything foolish—"

"The thing is," Antony told him, "I don't suppose either Cathie or her mother are loving me overmuch."

"*That* doesn't surprise me," said Conway, descending for a moment to the level of schoolboy repartee. Antony grinned at the telephone, but the frown was back between his eyes when he spoke again.

"Yes, but will you let me know?"

"I have already agreed." Not quite accurate, that. "Will you be at home?"

"I will."

"Very well, then. I'll be in touch," said Conway. And with that Maitland had to be content.

Sunday, 1st August

He was restless the next morning until Conway came, and rushed downstairs in a hurry when Gibbs announced the detective's arrival. "Come into the study, Inspector. It's my uncle's room, really, but he's out of town."

"I have been here before, Mr. Maitland," said Conway dryly.

"Yes, of course." He was talking for the sake of talking, and he knew it. Because he had asked Conway a question, and now he didn't want to hear the reply. But there was no avoiding it, of course. The Inspector followed him briskly, as though he had very little time to waste.

"I've been to see Mrs. Armstrong," he said as soon as the door was shut. "She tells me her daughter has disappeared."

Something he had known already, or was that to put the feeling in too clear a light. "When did she go?"

"A week last Friday. The twenty-third. She left a note to say she was going to her aunt's for the weekend, so Mrs. Armstrong didn't think anything of it until the Monday, when the girl didn't turn up to go to work. Then she had a look around and found that there was a suitcase missing, and a lot of her clothes—"

"Just like Molly Browne," said Antony. Conway gave a tight-lipped smile.

"It's what you were afraid of, isn't it? Except for the note, exactly like. The point is, you see, the aunt said she'd never been there; and it turned out she'd made the same excuse before, and with no more truth."

"Why on earth didn't Mrs. Armstrong tell you?"

"She said it didn't do much good before. In any event, it seems that the girl went of her own free will."

"So did Molly, and look what happened to her."

"The cases cannot be in any way parallel," said Conway severely. "However, it does occur to me, Mr. Maitland, that you may have some idea . . . some suggestion to make—"

This was so unlike the Inspector that for a moment Antony only stared at him. "I have a suggestion, of course. I think we ought to go down to Littlebourne without delay." Conway started to say something, but he ignored him and went on. "Yes, I know I shall have to convince you of that. Will you grant, at least, that it may be the place to which Molly Browne returned when she was 'resting'?"

"I won't argue with you."

"Well, I did get one bit of information from Miss Weaver that I thought was useless, but now I'm not so sure. Molly Browne once described to her the place where she'd lived with her husband; she said it was in Brightsea, but we're pretty sure that was a lie."

"You think you could recognize it?"

"A bungalow on the cliff top, 'the farthest from the town.' It would be different in Brightsea, but Littlebourne's such a tiny place, I think we could find it, all right."

"And what then?"

"With any luck we shall find Cathie Armstrong there, and Molly Browne's partner as well."

"I suppose," said Conway, with the familiar sarcasm back in his voice, "you're also going to tell me who the man is."

"I think I know." He would have left it there, but Conway was beginning to bristle. "We were talking the other day about who could have known the situation at Oakhurst."

"You made some quite unwarrantable assumptions."

"So I did. Well, here's one more. If Bill Stoddard had told his old friend Tom Kinglake—"

"Are you serious, Mr. Maitland?"

"Never more so. Kinglake's another old flame of Molly Browne; have you met him?"

"I have had no occasion—"

"He's a teacher," said Antony, rather as though that explained everything; and started to hunt through his pockets. "If you look at the list of dates we were given, you'll see it all fits in."

"What fits in?"

"With the school holidays. Everything that didn't happen then happened on a Saturday, as you pointed out."

"Is that all you have to go on?"

"No. Not really." He wasn't ready for all this, and if he was sure what Cathie's message meant . . . "There are other indications," he said unwillingly.

"What are they?"

"He's been keeping an eye on what I've been doing, under pretense of looking after Cathie. Then, he's the only person with a motive for attacking her *and* Geoffrey—"

"How do you make that out?"

"He never knew of the photograph you had of Molly . . . Mrs. Armstrong kept it in a drawer—remember?"

"I don't see—"

"Look at it from his point of view. First he thinks himself quite safe . . . the police may suspect the dead girl is Molly Browne, but after the work he's done on her face, they won't be able to prove it."

"Mr. Stoddard was an old friend of hers."

"So he was. But we've no reason to suppose he was in a position to know about the appendix scar, or the birthmark. Anyway, why should anyone ever ask him to view the body? When the identification was made, it was from a completely unexpected quarter . . . Cathie bullied her mother into going to the mortuary. Even then, he ought to have been safe enough, with a scapegoat ready to hand; but he was nervous, and when Cathie told him she'd had a long talk with me and I didn't believe the doctor was guilty, he got more worried than ever."

"Knowing your reputation, no doubt. *That* makes sense," said Conway unkindly.

"If you like. What he had to avoid now was the circulation of Molly Browne's picture, in case she was recognized under any of her aliases, so he tried to get hold of the snapshot, which he knew Cathie carried in her handbag. Your people in Streatham were quite right about that, you see . . . his main object wasn't to hurt her. It was only later that he learned from her that the snapshot was now in Horton's possession; and by that time, the postcard, which had also been handed to Geoffrey, was even more important to him. *I* told him about that, by the way, the first time he came to see me, the day before the attack on Geoffrey. Now do you see?"

"You're guessing, Mr. Maitland. Guessing rather wildly, if you will forgive me for saying so."

"For some reason or other, you seemed interested in my opinion," said Antony indifferently.

"You haven't explained why Molly Browne's body should have been buried in Dr. Langton's shrubbery."

"You're forgetting that, according to my theory, the murderer had been to Oak Dene before, on the occasion of Mrs. Langton's death. The garden has an atmosphere, you know . . . sinister in the extreme. It may have been no more than that that decided him. But if he wished to arrange for someone else to take the blame, you must admit he succeeded admirably." Conway only grunted. "There's another thing," said Antony, "and this won't convince you either. Kinglake's relationship with Molly Armstrong, when she was still living at home."

"What do you mean?"

"He'd made the tactical error of being accepted as a friend of the family . . . unromantic. He couldn't afford to take her out. He needed money, badly, to get her attention; still more, he needed something to make her see him in a different light."

"It seems rather drastic to have resorted to murder."

"I think we must accept that whoever committed the murders wasn't repelled by what he was doing. Cathie told me that when he attacked her he sounded as if he was excited. You wouldn't care to take up strangulation as a hobby, and neither would I—"

"You're saying that Molly Browne found it romantic."

"And so it was, in the sense that it was something completely remote from her own experience."

"And what about Cathie Armstrong, then?"

"I wish I knew. We've got to remember that Molly Browne was killed."

"What do you mean by that?"

"The murderer got rid of her, either because *she* got tired of the game they were playing, or perhaps because *he* got tired of her. In either case, it's a hundred to one he's got another partner now."

"That young girl!" Conway sounded shocked.

"He may have retired from business, he may only want a companion. In any event, I imagine he'd work up gradually to any disclosure he made. He may not think it would be too difficult to persuade her; she's in love with him, you see."

"The whole thing's fantastic."

"Yes, but you knew that, didn't you? It's no use trying to blame it all on me."

"I might have known how it would be," said Conway. He did not actually fling his arms to heaven, but he gave the definite impression of having done so. Antony smiled at him.

"The trouble with you, Inspector, is—you've got too nice a mind," he said.

"Seriously, Mr. Maitland—"

"Seriously, Inspector, I think it would be a good idea to find Cathie Armstrong, don't you?"

"The girl's of age. If she doesn't want to come home—"

"There's nothing to stop me from going. I may be said to have had an invitation, after all."

"But if you're right about the man—" That was three sentences that had gone uncompleted. Conway seemed to be in a most uncharacteristic state of indecision.

"At least I can give her the chance to come away if she wants to."

"You think he's keeping her there?"

"I think she's frightened. I don't know why." He glanced at his watch as he spoke, and said, suddenly in very much of a hurry, "If we go now, we can just catch the eleven-thirty from Victoria."

"But—"

"Look, Inspector, I'm not suggesting any impropriety. Come with me to Littlebourne. You can go to the local police station, see if they can tell you anything about the couple we're looking for. I'll join you there, with or without Cathie Armstrong. Right?"

"We don't even know—"

"She's with a man. I may be wrong about Kinglake, heaven knows I've been uncertain enough. But she didn't tell her mother lies to cover the fact that she was spending a week with a girl friend, now did she?"

"I suppose not. No."

"Come along, then. I've just got to tell Jenny." He was smiling to himself as he came down the stairs again with his raincoat over his arm. Jenny was so astonished that he should be going anywhere in Conway's company that it had never even occurred to her that the expedition might entail any risk.

/ 2 /

It wasn't quite as straightforward as that, of course. If he was right, there was bound to be some risk involved, but what worried him more than that was the risk to Cathie. He thought he had weighed the matter carefully, but whenever he decided that the pros, which were positive, outweighed the cons, which were problematical, some new aspect of the equation occurred to him, throwing him back into a state of indecision.

Conway seemed content to be silent during the journey; perhaps he was regretting his lost leisure, or brooding on the impulse that had led him to embark on so ill-conceived an expedition. He sat in the opposite corner of the carriage and looked disapproving, but that was nothing new. It was hot, and getting hotter; the only thing to be thankful for was that they were sitting on the shady side of the train.

Littlebourne is small, and considered dull by the masses, so that even at high summer there is only what might be regarded as a reasonable amount of overcrowding. Visitors are generally accommodated in the town, which remains unspoiled because of the high cliffs on either side; that is, if "unspoiled" means "cramped and inconvenient," as only too often it does.

They parted outside the station. Either Conway had been there before, or some sixth sense told him in which direction the police headquarters lay. Antony walked down a wide street toward the promenade. A noontide lethargy seemed to lie heavily over the town, complicated perhaps by the observance of the Sabbath. Nothing ever happened here, nothing could happen. . . .

When he reached the seafront he was willing to admit he had guessed badly; there was no sign of the bungalows that Molly Browne had mentioned. But when he had climbed the steep track to the west cliff, there they were before him, square, hideous, and undistinguished, but each with a superlative view. Looking back across the ravine, across the roofs of the town, he could see no similar signs of development to the east; anyway, here was the path, as Molly had said, and the road that ran behind the bungalows. And on the corner where it turned to circle the town, a small shop which, unlike the larger establishments he had passed, showed a hospitably open door.

He went into it mainly because he still hadn't quite made up his mind what to do. It seemed to sell everything. Antony bought a cellophane wrapped ham sandwich (with a passing qualm as to its age group), and a bottle of fizzy lemonade, because whatever else happened, he couldn't see Cathie offering him lunch. He lingered, looking at the postcards. And here again there was some sort of confirmation of what he believed . . . "The Promenade at Noon," with its impossibly blue sky, golden sands, and the girls in their bright, subtly old-fashioned dresses. He added it to his purchases, and began to feel in his pocket for change.

"I've been told," he said, "that there's a bungalow here for sale."

"Not that I've heard, there isn't," said the man behind the counter, rousing himself from the gloomy contemplation of his merchandise.

"A row of bungalows, not too close together, and this one is the farthest from the town," said Antony, quoting Miss Weaver's words as well as he could remember them.

"Oh, them! Summer people," said the shopkeeper, in a depressed tone.

"Only summer?"

"Well, no. Other times too. Weekends and such."

"Do you know the people?"

"Name of Baker. So I've *heard*." (From his tone, he didn't place much reliance on the information.) "Not that I see much of them; get what they want at the big shops, I wouldn't wonder. But they pass in the car now and then. Two of them, that's all I know."

"Mr. and Mrs. Baker?"

"That's as may be. Thought the girl looked different myself when she came in for a loaf the other day, but it wasn't no business of mine. Live and let live, that's what I say."

If he really meant that, there was at least a faint chance that the ham sandwich wouldn't prove actually lethal. Even so, Antony didn't think he'd risk it. He buried it in the ditch at the right side of the road, but he was thirsty enough to drink the lemonade, and then wished he hadn't. There were seventeen bungalows in all—he counted them—and he was hotter than ever when he reached the last one. There was no mistaking it, the unbroken turf of the cliff top stretched away beyond it as far as he could see. A place no more handsome than its neighbors, neatly kept, and with a newish, neat garage, the only one he had seen.

Shall I? Shan't I? As he walked, with his raincoat over his left arm, Sir Nicholas' automatic bumped encouragingly against his leg. A sensible precaution . . . that's what Uncle Nick had said when he procured the thing after a lively night two years ago. Antony wasn't so sure that Conway would agree with him. He stopped, and transferred the heavy pistol to a more convenient place in the pocket of his jacket; and thought that this action, too, was either sensible or impossibly dramatic, according to your point of view. Strangely enough, Henry Langton's affairs seemed to have lost their urgency; it was Cathie who occupied his mind. Cathie, who almost certainly wasn't the innocent she looked; who had written to him—inexplicably, insanely!—*Wish you were here.*

It was at this point that something occurred to resolve his doubts. A man came into view beyond the corner of the bungalow, who must have left it by a door at the back. He was dark, so much Antony could see, and he wore a yellow bathrobe; he made his way purposefully to the edge of the cliff, and disappeared from view where presumably a flight of steps led down to the sands below. Tom Kinglake? It was impossible to be sure. But at least the chances were that Cathie was alone.

He crossed the road, pushed open the gate, and started down the path. Rather a pleasant garden, full of color, which went a good way toward making up for the ugliness of the building. A green front door, with leaded panes primly curtained, and a knocker in the shape of a fish. He tried the bell instead, and almost immediately heard light footsteps crossing a wooden floor. He had one last moment of doubt before the door opened, but he had been right after all. It was Cathie Armstrong who stood there.

Whatever she had been expecting, his presence came as a shock to her. She had never had much color, but now she was paper white, and she backed away across the tiny hall with one hand over her mouth as though her first instinct had been to cry out. He followed until he had room to shut the door, and then leaned back against it. "Hello, Cathie," he said, watching her.

She lowered her hand then, but she still had a wary look. "I don't understand," she protested.

"You asked me to come," he pointed out. "At least, by implication."

"How did you know—?"

She broke off there and made no attempt to finish the sentence. "Birmingham by way of Beachy Head," he told her, and added irritably, seeing her expression become blank and uncomprehending, "I only mean that I took the long way around."

"What do you want?"

"I should be asking you that, Cathie. I thought perhaps you would let me take you back to town."

"But . . . I don't know."

"I doubt if we've time to argue the point. Tom has only gone for a swim, hasn't he? I don't suppose he'll leave you alone for long."

"So you know it was Tom. You saw him?" He nodded. That much was true, at least. "I don't know," she said again. "I don't know what to do."

"Come with me. If you're frightened—"

"Why should I be?"

"Why did you send me that postcard, if you weren't?"

"I didn't think . . . I didn't think you'd find me."

"You wanted me to know you were in Littlebourne. You wanted me to know that Molly had been here before you."

"Mr. Maitland, were they true . . . the things that were said about Molly at the trial?"

"I'm afraid they were."

She didn't say anything to that, just stood very still and looked at him with tragic eyes. He said after a moment, gently, "It isn't safe for you to be here. You know too much."

"I am frightened, of course, but that doesn't matter. I mean, if it were only that. I shouldn't mind dying," said Cathie, and he looked at her helplessly, because she was young enough to mean that now . . . at this moment . . . however much she might passionately *not* mean it in half an hour's time.

"If you won't care about yourself, think of your friends . . . think of your mother."

"It doesn't seem to make much difference to Mum whether she's glad or sorry. She's self-sufficient," said Cathie, momentarily as pleased to have found the right word as ever Sergeant Mayhew was over the appropriate platitude.

"You'll be telling me next she's over thirty," said Maitland, annoyed again.

"No. No." Unexpectedly she smiled at him. "I don't

know how you found us, but I think the best thing now would be for you to go away."

"You realize that if I do, I shall come back with the police."

"But then Tom would know—"

"What, Cathie? That you betrayed him?"

"I don't think you understand, Mr. Maitland." Her lip quivered, but she went on, clutching valiantly at the rags of her self-possession. "I couldn't do that, not really. Because I love him."

"But still, you wrote to me."

"I didn't mean . . . I didn't want . . . I didn't think you'd come here."

"Do you really want me to go away again?"

"Yes. No. I don't know." She glanced uneasily over her shoulder. "I don't believe you'd bring the police anyway. It's nothing to them, what I do."

"No," he admitted. "That's your own affair. But it does concern them who killed your sister, for instance. And Mrs. Ruth Langton, of course. And others."

"Others?"

"They seem to have worked about one job a year," said Antony, quoting.

"Since Molly left home? I don't believe you."

"Why did you send for me then?"

"Because . . . because . . . I wish I hadn't!"

"Cathie—"

"You don't know anything . . . you can't prove anything."

"—there's still Dr. Langton's point of view."

"He was acquitted." She said that quickly, but her eyes were anxious now.

"He's suffered a good deal over this, you know, and now his wife has left him."

"I didn't know *that*."

"No, but you guessed—didn't you?—how it might be. and that's why you sent the postcard."

"I don't know what you mean."

"A way of squaring your conscience," he said slowly.

"If I didn't respond, it would mean Tom wasn't meant to be found out."

"You're just making it up as you go along."

But he was sure now he had the answer, at least in part, to what she had done. Getting her to follow through on it was different matter, but dare he leave her here? If she blurted out to Kinglake when he came back to the bungalow . . .

"Why did you come here, Cathie?" he asked.

"Because I love him. I told you that."

"And you didn't know until you saw the postcards on sale—"

"I didn't know then," she said quickly, as though she didn't want to hear him complete the sentence. "I thought about it for days and days before I did anything, and even then I didn't *know*."

And there was still the matter of proof. If Cathie had none to give him . . . "You realized that Molly had stayed at Littlebourne, not at Brightsea, when she first left home. What made you so sure she had come here? Tom's secretiveness about the arrangement, perhaps—" He saw her eyes flicker as he brought out the suggestion, but was her expression one of relief?

"We aren't married," she said, as though that explained everything. "Tom doesn't believe in marriage, and neither do I."

"There must have been some other reason."

"No. Why should there be? I realized she must have stayed at Littlebourne, and I thought you'd be grateful to know that. The rest is just nonsense, something you made up."

"I'd better go then." And again he was in no doubt at all about her reaction. She was afraid. It showed in her eyes, in the quick movement of her hand—almost as though she would have clutched his sleeve—before she let it drop to her side again. "Cathie . . . come with me!"

He never knew whether that would have brought another denial. Perhaps it was some sound that had alerted him;

his hand went to his pocket, he turned his head to watch the doorway at the right of the little hall. Someone was crossing the room beyond, but the first thing he saw was a hand that reached out and grabbed roughly at Cathie's shoulder, pulling her sideways, until, when Tom Kinglake stood in the doorway, he was almost completely sheltered behind her body. Now his hands were around her throat.

"I'm not quite sure what's going on here," he said, "but it seems I got back just in time."

"Let her go," said Maitland. In the circumstances, the gun in his hand did not give him much of either comfort or confidence. Tom Kinglake smiled at him.

"In my own good time," he promised. (Oddly enough, the girl was standing passive, after the first gasp of fright, when her hands had flown up to scratch vainly at his. The thought crossed Antony's mind that they might have played this game before.) "When I've found out—" said Kinglake. "But meanwhile, I should drop that thing, if I were you. It's making me nervous."

"I, on the other hand, am happier in its possession."

"I don't see that. You can't do anything with it, except shoot Cathie, of course. I don't especially mind that, but I can't imagine what good it will do you."

"All the same—"

"Drop it, I said!"

"I think not."

"Unless you want to see me strangle Cathie. I can do it in a moment, you know; in fact, it would be a pleasure." His hands tightened a little, and again Antony saw the terror flare in the girl's eyes. "She has a lovely neck," said Kinglake. The words were like a caress.

"Don't—"

"I won't, if you're sensible. At least, not just yet. Not until I know—"

"You said yourself the gun's no use to me, as things are."

"Even so—"

Once before a threat had been made to him, very like

this. Then Jenny had been involved, and he hadn't hesitated; he shouldn't hesitate now. The pistol went down with a clatter. "That's better," said Tom, as though in congratulation. "Now push it toward me, with your foot."

There would be a moment, when Kinglake bent to retrieve it . . . but there wasn't, of course. What happened was that he gave Cathie a shove, so that she stumbled across the hall into Maitland's arms. By the time Antony had disentangled himself, Tom had the gun in his hand and was standing a little way back from the open door, well out of the range where it would have been reasonable to tackle him. "Now," he said, "we can talk in comfort."

"Have you ever fired a hand gun?"

"No gun of any kind. I've always wondered how I should make out with one. Don't give me an excuse to find out."

The disheartening thing was that the safety catch, which had been firmly on a moment before, was now indisputably in the firing position. "I won't," said Maitland, and meant it. There was very little room for maneuver here, but sooner or later he'd have to take a chance.

"The thing I want to know, of course, is what you're doing here. You mustn't think I'm not pleased to see you," said Kinglake, and strangely there was for a moment a measure of cordiality in his tone. "But I should like to know why you came; and how you knew we were here, for that matter."

"He came to see me, Tom," said Cathie clearly.

"Oh?" He looked from one of them to the other, and still it seemed no more than a polite inquiry.

"I sent him a postcard."

"With the *address*?"

"No. I just wanted him to know that Molly had stayed in Littlebourne. I never thought of him coming *here*."

"And I imagined that I should find you so amenable. It just goes to show that we're all liable to make mistakes," said Kinglake sadly. "But if you didn't tell him, my sweet—and don't think for a moment that I'm doubting you—how did he find this place?"

"He says he went to Birmingham," said Cathie in a

resentful tone. Antony thought it was time he took a hand.

"Not Birmingham . . . Carlington. Do you remember a certain Miss Weaver?"

"I never met her, of course. Molly spoke to her. But I still don't see—"

"It's a long story. Before I embark on it, I ought to tell you . . . the police know I'm here."

"Naturally," said Kinglake scornfully. "They're always so ready to believe any cock-and-bull story, aren't they? You've no proof. I know that."

"Do you? Your behavior since you came in just now—"

"Yes, but where are your witnesses? You don't think I can let you leave here alive, Mr. Maitland. As for Cathie, she must choose."

He thought she moved a little, closer to his side, but her voice was steady enough when she spoke. "What are the alternatives, Tom?" she asked.

"To put it bluntly, whether you live with me, or die with him."

She turned her head a little, looking up for a moment into Maitland's face. "I don't want to die," she said, very low.

"That's my good girl!" said Kinglake, with a heartiness that made Antony long to hit him. (But was he fool enough, or vain enough, to think he could trust her?)

"But first you must tell me . . . I've got to understand—"

"What do you want me to tell you?"

"Everything," said Cathie simply. "I love you, Tom. I've proved that, haven't I? So don't you think I have a right to know?"

"Don't talk to me about rights, Cathie."

"Is that what Molly did?"

"You're the last person to complain about what happened to her. I took you on, didn't I? Could I have done that if she were still alive?"

"So you killed her . . . for my sake?" Her mouth twisted a little, as though the thought displeased her, but her voice was level enough.

"Of course."

"And you killed Mrs. Langton too? I wish you'd tell me how it all began."

"It began, I suppose, because Molly didn't feel that the world would be well lost for love." His tone was quietly reminiscent. "And then one year on holiday I came across what would have been the perfect setup. There they were . . . prospective victim, a local contractor who had started running his business as if he had delusions of grandeur . . . his partner, the natural suspect, with a motive as big as a house. I began to see how it could have been worked, if I hadn't got to know both of them quite well in the meantime. It wouldn't have been safe, but if I had someone to help me . . . I realized at once that Molly would be ideal for the job, of course."

"But, Tom, you couldn't just say to her—"

"There was no need to say anything, except that I had a scheme for getting rich quick that needed her cooperation. She never realized what was involved until Kenneth Dekker was dead. The queer thing was, the reality didn't seem to shock her, or perhaps it was the money that turned the scale. I ought to have told her before; we nearly came to grief over that one. It turned out the wife had a lover, and if he hadn't happened to have an alibi too—"

"Would you have cared?"

"Of course I should. She'd have told the whole story, trying to protect him. But our luck held, and after that it was simplicity itself. We bought this place—I'd only rented it before—and the car that's in the garage; I don't suppose any of our neighbors realize that we don't take it when we leave. It isn't really far to walk into town along the sands. Molly was alone a little at first, until Easter, and then during the summer term, but after that we spent every holiday here together, and sometimes odd weekends too, and in between she was busy. She made a few false casts, of course, and had to move on to some other place—it's surprising, really, how many people *don't* want to murder their relations—but I must say we had a good deal of luck as well. It was a stimulating life, full of interest. There's nothing like having a purpose in what you do."

"And now you think that I—"

"No reason why not, Cathie. We'll go farther afield . . . Scotland, perhaps over to Ireland. We can have a good time together, you know that by now."

"Yes. Yes, I do."

"I was perfectly serious," said Maitland into the silence, "when I told you the police were interested in your activities. They know about Hutton Caldbeck, and Carlington, and Blackpool, and Colwyn Bay. I'm not sure if I've got those in chronological order—"

"It hardly matters. They're welcome to come here, for all I care." And, as though on a cue, Antony heard a very faint creaking sound—a door, or a french window, perhaps, being pushed open?—and a stealthy footfall on the carpeted floor. Someone who had come into the room behind Kinglake? He hadn't time to consider the implications. Tom was still speaking, and seemed to have heard nothing, but if once a silence developed . . . "I never showed myself at any of the places you mentioned, any more than I did at Oakhurst—"

"Tell me one thing. Did Dr. Langton know?"

"Before his wife died? No, of course not. Have you ever tried suggesting to somebody that it would be a good idea for you to commit a murder on their behalf? My way was safer. Foolproof, really. Because by the time they realized what had happened, you'd got them just where you wanted."

"I see." There was no sound now; he was almost sure he had been mistaken. "Molly Browne's connection with the crimes can be proved, however."

"It's a pity about that, but they've still to connect me with Molly."

"Easy enough, here in Littlebourne."

"If they know about this place, which I doubt. Even so, you'll not suggest the police would be interested in the moral aspect, I suppose."

"They would find the connection suggestive, now that they know so much."

"Don't try to scare me, Maitland. You, if anybody, should understand about the burden of proof."

"And—if it isn't an indiscreet question—what do you propose to do with me?"

"Shoot you, I suppose," said Tom carelessly.

"Apart from your desire to get in a little target practice, are you sure that's a good idea."

"If you're worried about my disposing of the body—"

"Not really."

"—it would be different if I believed anyone knew you were here. As it is, there's the sea . . . the garden . . . or perhaps I'll take you somewhere by car. There are lots of possibilities."

"And now you're suggesting that Cathie should take over where her sister left off."

"Why not?"

"She knows what happened to Molly. Do you think you could trust her?" This might be a dangerous line to take, but he had to get the girl's attention somehow. He turned to her as he spoke. "What about it, Cathie?" And her eyes moved to meet his at the precise moment that Inspector Conway came into sight behind Kinglake's shoulder.

"I don't want to die, Mr. Maitland," said Cathie composedly, as she had done before. And suddenly he realized that she had been talking to gain time, just as surely as he had been doing; that she was playing to his lead now as well as she could, though he doubted if she understood what was happening.

He put a hand under her chin, holding her so that she could no longer turn her head, and said lightly: "The children of this world are wiser in their generation than the children of light."

As before, the quotation seemed to make her uneasy; he could feel her straining against his restricting hand. It was all he could do not to look around himself; every nerve was on edge, because when Conway acted, as it seemed he must act . . .

He felt, rather than saw, the Inspector's movement. There was only one way to go, and that was toward the stairs, and he took Cathie with him so that they finished up in a heap with her underneath. He felt her go limp as he heard the shot, but he didn't think she could . . . possibly have been hit. He scrambled to his feet and saw Kinglake with the gun pointing harmlessly at the floor, and Conway hanging on to his arm; and went, a little breathlessly, to the detective's assistance.

/ 3 /

They took stock later, in the train going back to town. Tom Kinglake had safe lodging with the local police, until arrangements could be made to have him moved; and Cathie had been sent home hours ago in an ambulance, though she had come around so quickly after hitting her head as she fell that the doctor didn't think there could be any concussion. "We've got him now," said Conway, on a note of complacency. "And everything tied up neatly . . . thanks to you."

"If we're to talk of gratitude," said Antony, "I'd be dead by now if it wasn't for you."

"So I heard. I was sorely tempted," said Conway, "to delay my intervention. But it wouldn't have done, I suppose. Someone might have asked questions."

"So they might. How disappointing for you," said Antony, and grinned at him. Five minutes of violent action while Tom Kinglake was subdued seemed to have had an effect out of all proportion on the Inspector, whom he had never known before to essay even the mildest pleasantry. "For the rest of it, though . . . do you think Cathie Armstrong will come up to proof?"

"There's the ring she found . . . the thing she says convinced her, because she knew it was her sister's. Mrs. Armstrong can just as well identify that, I suppose."

"It would come better from Cathie."

"So it would. But there's Molly Browne's diary too."

"What in heaven's name possessed him to keep it?"

"It wasn't exactly incriminating in itself—"

"Anyway, I don't suppose he *kept* it, exactly, just didn't bother to throw it away."

"—but even the entry '*Tom coming tomorrow*' will be

helpful in confirmation of the facts we already have," said Conway, with a partial return to his normal severity. But he added, with deep satisfaction, "Once you know where to look, there's always evidence."

"Always?"

"Well . . . often. Now, you tell me, Mr. Maitland . . . would Miss Armstrong have gone along with him as her sister did?"

"No. No, I'm almost sure she wouldn't. I think she will give her evidence, too, as promised, and I think it will hurt her terribly."

"That can't be helped, I'm afraid."

"Funnily enough, I don't think it's the murders that shock her so much as the fact that someone else might suffer for them; and I'm not saying that means she might have condoned murder herself. But between you, you should be able to clear Dr. Langton . . . don't you think? You heard what Kinglake said."

"I did. And I realized when I heard you prompting him that you knew I was coming."

"Which brings me to another question, Inspector. Why weren't you at the police station?"

"I wanted to see what kind of trouble you might be getting yourself into, and it didn't seem to me there was much I could usefully say to the local people at that stage."

"You don't mean—you can't mean, Inspector—that you effected an arrest in someone else's manor without so much as by-your-leave?"

"It went against the grain, I can assure you, Mr. Maitland."

"And then we finally delivered our prisoner tied up like a bundle of laundry." But the detective made no other reply to this than a slight compression of the lips.

There could be no doubt about it now; as far as Detective Inspector Conway was concerned, the honeymoon was over.